What the Dog Said

What the Dog Said

Randi Reisfeld

with HB Gilmour

BLOOMSBURY

NEW YORK BERLIN LONDON SYDNEY

First published in the United States of America in February 2012
by Bloomsbury Books for Young Readers
www.bloomsburykids.com

For information about permission to reproduce selections from this book, write to
Permissions, Bloomsbury BFYR, 175 Fifth Avenue, New York, New York 10010

Library of Congress Cataloging-in-Publication Data
Reisfeld, Randi.
What the dog said / by Randi Reisfeld with HB Gilmour. — 1st U.S. ed.
p.   cm.
Summary: Shortly after their police officer father is killed in the line of duty,
thirteen-year-old Grace's older sister decides to adopt a dog to train as a
service dog for a handicapped child so that she can write about it for her
college applications, but, true to form, it is the grief-stricken Grace who
ends up taking responsibility for the dog.
ISBN 978-1-59990-702-4 (hardcover)
[1. Grief—Fiction.   2. Dogs—Training—Fiction.   3. Human–animal
communication—Fiction.   4. Fathers—Fiction.   5. Sisters—
Fiction.]   I. Gilmour, HB (Harriet B.)   II. Title.
PZ7.R277457Wh 2012   [Fic]—dc23   2011026031

Book design by Nicole Gastonguay
Typeset by Westchester Book Composition
Printed in the U.S.A. by Quad/Graphics, Fairfield, Pennsylvania
2 4 6 8 10 9 7 5 3 1

This book is dedicated to the memory of HB Gilmour.
I hope I've done you proud, my friend.

He wasn't the most courageous of dogs. Nor, it must be said, was [he] very bright. But he was loyal beyond measure and knew what mattered. Din-din, walks, balls. But most of all, his family. His heart filled his chest and ran to the end of his tail and the very tips of his considerable ears. It filled his head, squeezing out his brain. But [the dog] . . . while not particularly clever was the smartest creature [his owner] knew. Everything he knew he knew by heart.

—LOUISE PENNY, *Bury Your Dead: A Chief Inspector Gamache Novel*

What the Dog Said

·· 1 ··

Dog Picks Girl

Cages. A prison grid of cells. Dogs sniffing, baying, circling frantically inside them. I didn't want to be there. Reluctantly, I followed my sister along the corridor between the cages, my heart racing, my senses scrambled by the fretful sounds echoing off the concrete walls and floor and by the sickly sweet stench of perfumed cleaning solvent, wet fur, and desperation.

I bowed my head, barely restraining the impulse to put my hands over my ears. My thick auburn hair fell forward, hooding my face. Inside my zippered sweatshirt I was shivering, but my hands were sweating. I wiped them on my jeans.

Coming to the shelter was a bad idea, I thought again, unable to focus on any one animal, seeing only motion, hearing above the din the anxious clacking of nails on concrete. Why had I let my mom talk me into going with Regan to, of all things, adopt a dog?

Because Mom thought it would help. Make me feel better. Because I needed to think about something other than myself. Other than my dad, she meant. I needed to uncoil the knot of loss inside me, to unlock the dark cell I'd been living in since Dad died.

Regan agreed. She couldn't wait until I got "back to normal." How could she not see that normal died the day our dad did? I mean, I know Regan suffered, too, but in most ways, she's back to acting like her old self. When I'm feeling charitable toward her, I think it's because she's sixteen, and she got to love Dad three years longer than I did. When I'm feeling less generous, I think it's because she's too self-absorbed to care about anybody else.

"A dog?" I'd sputtered, outraged. "You think getting a dog will help me 'get over it'?"

"That's part of the reason," Mom had conceded.

Wrong. We both knew—all three of us knew—the bigger reason. It was about Regan. And Regan's need to create perfection, in this case, a perfect essay that would get her into college. She's only a junior, but she's determined to have her early-decision application submitted in September, less than six months from now. Regan believed that an essay about training a shelter puppy to become a service dog would make her look better than other applicants. She'd already hooked up with a sponsor organization called Canine Connections. They'd actually approved Regan—us—as official volunteers.

"We can train him together. It'll be a sisters' project!" she'd said brightly.

Translation: "You can walk and feed and clean up after him. Most likely, you'll end up with the training part, too."

This dumping of chores really isn't mean-spirited. She was born that way. Whenever Regan takes on a project with another person, it's usually the other one who does the heavy lifting. Regan inevitably has something more urgent to do, and she always promises to "make it up to you." I fully believe she means it at that moment—only somehow, the "makeup time" never seems to arrive.

When I pointed this out, Regan's comeback was that this project was *her* doing *me* a favor. "You've been hiding out in your room for nearly six months," was her justification. "This will force you out."

"I go out," I'd countered.

"To school. And then you're back home, not answering your phone, hardly ever coming down to eat, not letting Jasmine or even Mercy into the house. You don't talk to anyone."

I'm embarrassed, I'd wanted to say, but I was shocked

to even think it. Like Regan would understand. Okay, I didn't understand it myself, not really; the hot shame that surrounded my sorrow because Dad was dead, gone like a part of me, like a leg, leaving me lopsided, crippled.

I didn't cry.

I wished I could grieve like a normal person, instead of feeling abandoned and—and guilty. With a fist, I rubbed the end of my nose. My eyes were close to tearing, but I knew it was from the cold, and not the unfathomable loss. Why do they keep these shelters so frigid?

"Grace." Regan's voice rose over the chaos in the cages, echoing along the concrete hallway. "I think I found him! He's soooo cute! He looks smart, too!"

Obediently, I looked at the white fluffball dog Regan was pointing to. "He looks just like a Malti-poo!" she crowed. "That's what Sheena has!"

Sheena Weston, queen of the high school jungle, is Regan's cohort in fabulousness.

"No, no, no. Pick me!"

I spun around. In the cage behind me, a dog sat posing as if for a portrait of canine good humor and fidelity. His shaggy gray muzzle seemed strained into something resembling a smile.

"Did you hear that?" I asked Regan.

"She didn't," the dog assured me, standing now, his tail wagging like a hairy propeller. "You're the only one who can."

Right. Why not add hearing voices and talking dogs to the list of what's wrong with me?

"What?" Regan said distractedly. She was consulting a phone app for a list of "smartest dogs," a leading criteria in her search.

"I'm smarter than your average designer dog," bragged the gray-and-brown mutt, glancing nervously at my sister, who was still some feet away. "The snowflake only looks sweet and adorable, but take it from me, she's a real diva. You'll be waiting on her before you know it! So hurry and pick me first, okay? You won't be sorry, you'll see. Oh, please, girl. Please, Stace—"

"Grace," I corrected him without thinking.

"What?" Regan turned away from the petite, pure white ball of cuddliness to the ungainly, unkempt, prickly coated mutt with the lopsided grin. You could picture one jumping into your arms—the other knocking you over. One you'd carry in a designer bag. The other might eat one.

I don't know what came over me, but suddenly I heard myself say, "How about this one?" I swallowed hard. "I mean, he's kind of cute."

"You're kidding, right?" said Regan seriously.

"You shouldn't say that in front of him," I whispered. "It might . . . I don't know . . . hurt his feelings."

"No, no, no," the dog said. "I'm used to it. I try, but what can I do? I'm not the best-looking dog on the cell block." He chuckled. "She doesn't know you can hear me. This is between us."

"It might hurt his *feelings*?" Regan asked, waiting for me to let her in on the joke.

I searched Regan's flawless face. Her dazzling blue eyes were like perfectly round twin swimming pools. My own eyes were hazel, as dappled green and brown as a Florida lagoon, my dad used to say.

The dog was right. My sister hadn't heard him say anything. Which meant that I was . . . crazy. *Snap out of it*, I lectured myself sternly. *Dogs can bark and whimper and occasionally make yowling noises some people describe as singing, but they do not speak words—not in English or any other human language. Dogs don't talk. Only crazy people think they do.*

I meant to turn away from the pleading pup, but instead I took a step closer and grabbed the plastic sleeve hooked to his cage. His name was Rex. Something kept me rooted to the spot. Something like trembling excitement.

I looked up at Regan, who, unlike me, was tall and perfectly proportioned. Regal was her nickname at school. She was still staring at me, wondering if her little sister had toppled over the edge of sanity.

I felt my pale, freckled face flush. I forced myself to smile as if I'd just been kidding. My smile was so rusty, I was surprised that it didn't hurt. More surprised that I was pressing my case for the mutt.

"I kinda like this one, Regan. Maybe he's not Malti-poo cute," I conceded, purposely pronouncing the breed as if it were a disease. "But look at his sturdy build and noble muzzle and intelligent eyes. He's tall, so he's definitely got some Lab in him, some shepherd, too. I bet there's even a trace of poodle, and I definitely see Border collie; that's the canine Einstein! Regan, we'll get him trained in no time."

Totally made all that up.

Regan scrunched her nose, then tilted her head, considering. Of the two of us, Regan might be the striver-conniver, but I'm the smart one.

"Excellent," cheered the big, scraggly dog who may or may not have had any of those forebears. "Did you fill out the papers?" He was sitting again, looking up at my sister and preening as if he were trying to impress her. "They're going to close soon and there are about a hundred forms to fill out before they'll let a dog out of here," he told me, while he tried out his lopsided grin on Regan. "You can't even spring a hamster without filling out forms. And you've got to pay up, too. The dog your sister was hot for, he's two hundred and fifty bucks. I'm your basic bargain on account of being not-that-cute, or—keep this between us—a little past my puppy years. Anyway, I'll be a lot less."

Looking doubtful, Regan scrolled through her cell phone info. She frowned. "It does say Labs are usually chosen for their devotion to their masters. Yellow Labs and German shepherds are the seeing-eye guide dog of choice."

"And everyone knows poodles are brilliant—that's why there are so many combinations, Labradoodles, Goldendoodles, Aussiedoodles." I was laying it on kinda thick.

"Well, okay, you're probably right," Regan said. "But how do we really know this guy is any of those mixes?"

I rolled my eyes. "Just look at him!" I practically sputtered.

Or don't, I thought, getting nervous.

He was big. He was goofy looking. He was . . .

"So not cute." Regan pouted.

"So what?" I said, feeling a tinge of . . . what? Betrayal? To a random dog? "It's not like he's staying. After we train him, you're giving him away, right? Isn't that the whole point?"

And so it was a done deal. As we sprung Rex from

the shelter, the weirdness of the moment hit me. My mom and sister thought my coming here would help me get back to normal. Instead, I heard a dog talk. I think that's either irony or payback.

·· 2 ··

Moving In

Back when the world was real, my mom would have sent Rex packing moments after he got home. Even though she'd signed the consent forms allowing us to adopt the dog by ourselves, Mom retained veto power. If our choice was unacceptable, he'd be gone. Obviously Rex didn't know this, because he didn't exactly put his best paw forward. In his delirium about being adopted, he hurtled into our house at warp speed, dragging me, his leash, and the bag of dog food I was carrying in his wake. Rex raced through the mudroom and, like a heat-seeking missile, honed in on the living room, which he explored frantically. That's when the phrase "bull in a china shop" really came alive for me.

I don't think he meant to be destructive, but his hyper-passionate personality got the best of him, turning him into a weapon of canine mass destruction. Everything once stationary got swept in the air and crash-landed on the shiny new hardwood floor. That included every item on the coffee table, the fanned-out magazines, a mug of tea (which, wouldn't you know it, was half full), a tangle of TV remotes. The glass bowl filled with tangerines, apples, and grapes wasn't spared. Rex showed no remorse. He didn't realize his ginormous tornado-tail had caused it all.

"Rex, no!" I yelled, mentally totaling up the damage. "Regan, a little help here!" I was already on my hands and knees picking shattered glass up off the floor. My sister, big surprise, was oblivious, texting her friends about our new arrival.

I caught a glimpse of Mom struggling to compose her face. The old Mom, an organizational wiz and neat freak, would have banished Rex on the spot. Mom 2.0, the one she turned into after Dad died, did not shout, scold, punish, or criticize. Which is probably some rule for dealing with grief-stricken teenagers she got from one of her bereavement books.

She choked out, "Are you sure he's . . . trainable? He's awfully bulky. And . . . disruptive."

Words came out of my mouth without so much as a pause in my brain. "He's not really like this. He's probably nervous and excited. New home and all . . ." I trailed off.

I didn't stop to wonder why I was defending Rex, or even why I'd felt compelled to adopt him in the first place. Then again, thinking I heard him talk? Reason was not my strong suit right then.

"Are you sure he's clean? He looks—"

"Like something a monkey dragged in?" Regan, finally off the phone, finished for her.

"He's totally housebroken," I claimed, though I knew no such thing. I stole a glance at Rex, messily chomping on an apple.

"Tell her I don't shed . . . much."

I raised my eyebrows in disbelief. *Tell her yourself*, I wanted to say.

"But isn't he kind of . . . big? How much does he weigh?" Mom's voice was quavery.

I mumbled, "Maybe fifty pounds?" The adoption papers clearly had him twenty pounds more.

"Has he had his shots?" Mom asked, raking her fingers through her tangle of honey-blond curls.

"All his papers are in order," I told her. At least that much was true.

"And you picked this dog out . . . both of you?" Translation: *Regan has better taste.*

My sister shrugged. "Grace insisted."

Rex must have sensed Mom's distrust, and possible betrayal from Regan. He rose and trotted over to my mom. He sat at her feet and offered up his paw. Which is cute, especially when a dainty dog does it. Not so much Rex, whose oversize clumsy claw accidentally came down on her thigh and ripped a hole in her jeans.

Here's the part where Mom, even this new Zen-Mom, should have freaked. A grimace crossed her face, but amazingly, she held it together. Attempted to brush it off even. "Never liked how these jeans fit anyway."

She must have really been worried about me.

~

THE GANG'S ALL HERE! is the cheery caption above the photo. The four of us, Mom, Dad, Regan, and I, look like sausages stuffed into shiny black wet suits. The photo was from two summers ago. We were posed beside a neon-orange rubber raft, about to ride the rapids on the Colorado River. I was squinting into the sun, looking doubtful. Regan was doing her best I-can-rock-a-wet-suit pose. Mom looked hopeful. Dad was beaming.

WE ARE FAMILY! proclaims the next caption, angled jauntily over a shot of us in the actual raft. Regan and Mom were perched in the back, my dad and I up front. We all held paddles, but in true Abernathy family form, Dad and I did most of the work.

Memories. Page after scrapbook page, picture after picture. Each one told a story. And each story ended with a stab in the pin cushion my heart had become. After bringing Rex home, I was doing exactly what Regan accused me of, shutting myself up in my room, not taking calls or texts, or doing homework. I was surrounding myself with proof that life wasn't always this lonely. That I hadn't always hurt this much.

It didn't make me feel better, but I don't deserve to anyway.

This had become a nightly ritual. Except tonight, of course, was different. I had a new cell mate in my self-imposed exile. The dog was inspecting everything, making loud sniffing noises, burying his snout and pawing through the piles of clothes, books, papers, crusted plates, and random leftovers that littered the floor. Regan called my room a toxic dump site, but the mess didn't bother me. Nor Rex, apparently.

"I'm so happy! I love this room! I love your bed! Can I come up here? Please. Please, please, please!" His front paws, a silty gray with surprisingly snowy-white tips, had already edged the bedspread. I'm guessing service-dogs-in-training shouldn't be jumping on furniture, but this one didn't know what he was in for yet. He took my non-answer as a yes.

I flipped forward in the scrapbook until I found the pictures from last summer. We only ever took real vacations once a year, and unsurprisingly, Regan and I had lobbied for dramatically different destinations. My sister wanted New York City, because it's sophisticated, the fashion center of the world, because her pal Sheena allegedly saw Sarah Jessica Parker in an organic foods emporium there—because they actually *have* organic foods emporiums there. New York, New York, the opposite of boring old Jupiter, Florida. Also because Regan's ultimate dream is to be a fashion designer and her dream college, the Parsons School for Design, is there. My sister is nothing if not pragmatic.

Meanwhile, I had an amazing trip planned. We'd go out west for a hiking and camping trip in Bryce Canyon or Zion National Park. Then I wanted to go to a Navajo Native American reservation and see Four Corners Monument. It's the only place in the USA where the borders of four states—Arizona, Colorado, New Mexico, and Utah—intersect. There's this spot where you lie down and put one foot and one arm each in a different state. How cool is that? I don't think that makes me a nerd.

Plus, my dad and I had this plan: before I turned twenty-one, we were going to visit every Major League Baseball stadium in the US. So far, I've seen the Florida Marlins and the Atlanta Braves. By going out west, we could hit the Colorado Rockies baseball stadium and the Arizona Diamondbacks. That'd be four out of thirty. And I was only twelve.

True, if we went to New York, we could see Yankee Stadium and Citi Field, where the New York Mets play. But going out west would be much better!

Our sister battle for vacation dominance got fierce. I accused Regan of total self-absorption, and she accused me of terminal nerdiness.

My mom tried to make peace by researching a third choice that would satisfy both of us—and fit into our budget.

Dad settled it.

"We're doing both," he announced one night as he came home from work, practically blasting through the door. Before anyone could react, Dad explained, "I've decided to take two weeks this year. We'll spend one in New York, then go out west."

We were stunned into silence. Two weeks? Unheard of! Dad was a detective with the West Palm Beach Police and also worked with at-risk teenagers. Summer, when we took our vacations, was when troubled kids were most at risk—Dad couldn't spare much time away. Plus, the expense of two places, two thousand miles apart? Had he just gotten a raise?

Or had he known, somehow, that this would be the last vacation we'd ever take as a family?

Maybe if I concentrated hard enough on the pictures, I'd find a clue. Only concentrating on anything was difficult as Rex, cozily ensconced at the foot of the bed, continued to babble away. Not that he was really talking, but apparently the shut-off valve in my head was faulty.

"I'm so glad you picked me. You won't be sorry. I'll be good. By the way, I love what you've done with the room! That wall you painted black speaks volumes—genius!"

Maybe if I ignore him, I'll stop hearing him.

My phone, sitting on the nightstand, vibrated. I ignored that, too.

Rex picked his head up, looking from me to the phone. "Aren't you going to answer that?"

"La-la-la-la-la," I actually sang with my fingers in my ears. Not. Hearing. Him.

"What if it's important?" Rex now inched his way toward the nightstand, nosing at the still-vibrating phone.

I grabbed it and turned it off.

"Shouldn't you be doing your homework? I bet you have some."

I shook my head. Not because I didn't have homework. I shook my head in disbelief, because I'd like not to be crazy. And hearing a dog talk—and make perfect *sense*—qualifies.

"You did the right thing picking me, you know." Rex kept up his banter. "Imagine if you'd gotten stuck with that furry blob?" He shivered. "I do not think she'd be keeping you such excellent company right now."

I heard a growl. It was coming from me. "Listen, dog—"

"Call me Rex."

"Okay, Rex. I know you can't really understand me, and you're not really talking . . . but do me a favor, I'm right in the middle of something. So, please—" I was about to say "shut up," when just then the door banged open.

It was too much to expect Regan to knock, but barging in is harsh, even for her.

"That's strange," she mused, posing in the doorway. "Your phone is over there, your laptop is off, no earbuds. Yet I heard noise—like someone talking."

I reddened.

"That was the TV. I just shut it," I lied.

My sister wasn't all that bright, but even she could tell when I was lying. She shrugged. "Whatever. Just came to remind you that we have to sign him"—she gazed over at Rex and shuddered—"up for classes."

"And by we, you mean me."

"I've got an art club meeting after school and you've got . . . what? A long afternoon of wallowing in front of you?"

I threw a pillow at her. But not before she got in last licks. "It's putrid in here—open a window at least!"

Later, as I drifted off to sleep, I tried again to give

myself a reality check, make sense of the nonsensical. Dogs can communicate with humans, but they don't talk.

They do, as I found out, snore.

I think I prefer the talking.

··3··

First Licks

I loooove you. I loooove you."

Of course Rex didn't say that. But I swear that's what I heard as his slobbery tongue swiped my chin, lips, and nose over and over again. Combined with his hot doggy breath, it was more than enough to gross me out of the deepest sleep. I also didn't need a sharp-clawed paw digging into my shoulder. I rolled away from him and pulled the blanket over my head.

The tongue—and the dog attached to it—would not be denied. Within seconds, Rex had hoisted his whole self onto the bed and his moist muzzle found its way underneath the quilt. He continued to treat my face like an ice-cream cone.

"Stop it!" I scolded, tucking my chin down and curling into a ball so he couldn't get me.

"Gotta go! Walk me! Walk me *now*. Come on, get up, gotta go!" Rex was panting.

I opened one eye and slid it toward the bedside clock. 6:02. Ugh.

Blearily, I stumbled down the hallway and through the kitchen, trailing Rex. Mom was already up and online, gulping what I suspected was last night's reheated coffee and picking at a still-frozen bagel. The thought hopscotched across my muddled mind: Had she even slept?

"You're walking him?" Mom asked with a frown.

"I'm pretty sure he's got to go," I replied.

"Look, Grace, I see this dog has already taken a shine to you—but you and Regan should share the responsibility."

We should? I thought this was Regan's deal, and I'm just being the sap I usually am. I was about to challenge Mom when Rex interrupted. That is, the doggy-voice in my head sounded urgent.

"Ixnay on the chitchat. When a guy's gotta go, he's gotta go! My leash is on the peg in the mudroom. Let's go—Race!"

"Grace."

"What did you say?" Mom asked.

"Nothing," I mumbled. "I'm already up. I'll get Regan to walk him later."

Later, as in most likely, never.

~

Regan drives me to school. Although she got her license when she turned sixteen, Regan didn't always have a car. Mom used to drop us both off—first Regan at Jupiter High School, then me at Jupiter Middle. The two schools, about a mile apart, are conveniently on the way to Palm Beach Community College, where Mom is Professor Judith Abernathy, Chairperson, Department of Mathematics.

Mom drove a swanky (for us) SUV; Dad, a cranky Ford Fiesta. When our lives got upended last November, Mom gave the big car to Regan, on the grounds that it was bigger-meaning-safer. "I'll keep Dad's car until it dies," she'd reasoned. I knew she regretted her choice of words right then.

Dad would not have approved. He would not have wanted Regan in an expensive car. The girl drives like the ditz-diva she is, more interested in being seen than seeing the road. Riding shotgun with Regan means being her eyes and ears—if you want to live.

"Remember, Grace," she said the Monday after we got Rex, "today's the first training day for that dog. He's got to be certified as a full-fledged service dog by the time my college essay is due, so it's crucial to be at all the classes, and to be on time."

"What do you mean all the classes?" I bristled. "After today, you're taking him."

"Of course." She waved me away dismissively. "Let's take one day at a time. And today I need you to be outside the school right after last period. Mom will pick you up; you'll get the dog and take it to Canine Connections on Military Trail. Clear?"

My sister excels at delegating. Which beats actually doing anything herself. Weirdly, I don't hate her for being both beautiful and manipulative. She's got other good qualities. Which escape me at the moment.

"Hey, Grace." Jasmine Richards and Kendra Ramirez sidled up to me in the hallway. Ever since grade school they, along with Mercy Goldstein, have been my closest, most trusted friends. They acted like they still were.

It was admirable, their loyalty, since I'd given them every reason to drop me. How many more "missed" phone calls, deleted messages, and turned-down invites would it take until they got the real message?

It's nothing against them. I just couldn't force myself to care about the things they did, like classes, the eighth-grade dance, the yearbook, midterms, and least of all, who posted what about whom.

Even if I could pretend to care, it'd be so wrong, on so many levels.

"We've got practice this afternoon." Jasmine tried to

sound casual, while stating the obvious. Why else would they be wearing their Jupiter Middle School softball uniforms? Cleats with knee-high socks aren't trendoid Jazz's footwear of choice.

"You could come," Kendra said carefully. "Just hang out."

"Maybe," I lied. No way would I ever set foot on that softball field again.

"So what'd you do this weekend?" asked perky Kendra, who'd clearly spent hers at the beach. Her sunburned face and bronzed arms stood out against her blue, yellow, and white softball tunic.

"We got a dog."

"And you didn't tell me?" Jasmine was indignant. "I called you, like, seventeen times." Jazz has to be the first to know everything. She's the source of whatever goes viral at school, and she doesn't like coming in second when there's a newsblast. She uploads, texts, and tweets incessantly. Yep, she is that girl.

"She can tell us now," Kendra said brightly. Kendra dislikes conflict, even when it's minuscule, even when it doesn't involve her: she's the smoother-over.

"There's not much to tell. It's for Regan. She's going to train him to become a service dog."

Kendra blinked in disbelief. Jasmine's jaw fell open.

"It's for her college application," I clarified. "So it'll look good."

"And yet we all know who's getting stuck with the training." Mercy came bouncing along just then, diving as seamlessly into the conversation as an Olympian slices into a lap pool. "Your sister is just like my brother Raj: do-nothings."

"No, that's not it."

That's exactly it, but the instinct to defend my sister is a reflex—albeit a gag reflex sometimes.

Normally, Mercy would debate this. But now she simply looked at me with sad brown eyes. Even my best friends, even now, six months after it happened, didn't know how to act around me. It's like they were afraid if they contradicted me over anything I'd fall apart. It's not like I'd done anything to make them think any differently.

"What does the puppy look like?" Jasmine wanted to know. "All kinds of adorable?"

"He's . . . intelligent-looking," I answered. "Which, for Regan's purposes, trumps adorableness." I omitted the full description, as well as the most salient fact about Rex. Although if I really wanted my friends to dump me, telling them I hear the dog talk might just do the trick.

As I slid into my seat in language arts, I pictured what Rex was doing right then. Only his third day home, and left alone in an empty house. Was he stretched out, muzzle resting on his paws, eyes wide and glued to the front door waiting for someone to come home? Was he missing me?

"Don't worry about me," Rex had assured me that morning.

"What makes you think I would worry?" I'd been distracted enough to actually talk back to him (!) while trying to locate the least-ratty-looking jeans from the epic mess on the floor.

Rex had tilted his scraggly head and looked me square in the eye. It was like he knew exactly what I was feeling.

I had bigger problems right then. Bigger, as in, the jeans I'd just pulled up slid down to my ankles. I frowned. This wasn't good. But how was I supposed to have an appetite when everything tasted like chalk?

An idea for a diet plan struck me. The grief diet! Lose someone you love and watch those pounds melt away! Without thinking, I reached for my phone. I always told Jazz or Mercy my bizarre ideas, but something told me they wouldn't get my strange humor on this one.

"Can I borrow a pair of jeans?" I'd stuck my head into Regan's room. My size-zero sister was half dressed, texting away like a madwoman while talking into the landline, wedged between her cheek and neck. She waved me toward her closet. When she's motivated, Regan can be just as organizationally obsessive as my mom. As a fashion-designer-in-waiting, clothes and accessories fall into that category. Everything in her closet is arranged according to hue and size, coordinated seasonally and by trend. "The bigger sizes are in the back," she called out. "Take a pair that cuffs at the ankle."

"I'm going to explore today!" Rex had continued talking as though I hadn't even left the room. "But don't worry, no belongings will be injured or harmed during my walkabout. I'll just sniff. No tail action."

"You should probably stay away from Regan's room," I heard myself warn the dog that was in fact Regan's dog.

"I'm troubled, Grace." Mr. Kassan jolted me from my morning replay to the here and now. Uh-oh. Our language arts teacher was handing back exam papers from our "Coming of Age" unit. The test, a combination essay and multiple choice, covered everything we'd discussed and read—or should have—for the past two months.

"Please see me after class," he instructed.

"Sure," I mumbled, eyeing the packet of papers in front of me. I knew I'd blown the test, but whatever. I flipped through the exam booklet to see exactly how bad it was, but the pages were devoid of any marks. The exam was ungraded. A hot flush of shame crept from my neck to my face. It was ungraded because my teacher hadn't wanted to fail me. His kindness made me hurt all over.

At the end of the period, I approached Mr. Kassan's

desk. Too embarrassed to look at him, I averted my eyes. I wished I could tell him that being pitied is worse than being failed.

Thankfully, he didn't start out with the default, "I know you've been through a lot . . ." I gave him silent kudos for that.

He also scored points for not taking the "help me help you" route. He simply said, "Of the books on the reading list, I hoped you'd choose *To Kill a Mockingbird*, or *The Pigman & Me*. I had the feeling you could bring some new insights to the classic Harper Lee story—and I wanted to see what you'd make of *The Pigman*."

I hadn't picked either. Instead, I'd recycled Regan's old paper on *A Separate Peace*. I knew it probably wasn't very good; some part of me knew that Mr. Kassan would realize I'd neither read the book nor written the paper, but I didn't care.

Why should language arts be different than any of my other classes? Just showing up takes everything I've got.

"I know this seems meaningless to you now," he said, thankfully without forcing me to look at him. "But I promise you will feel differently later. So here's what we're doing to do. We're going to table this exam. We're going to act like it didn't happen. In a week, or a month, or whenever you decide you're ready to redo it, we'll come back to it."

"I don't know when I'll be ready," I mumbled, anxious to leave.

"Back in September when we went over the syllabus, you told me you were looking forward to this unit— remember?"

Back in September the world was still spinning on its axis. Back in September, I didn't know that in less than three months my father would be gone. Or that it would be my fault.

Canine Connections

Dogs. Circling, canting, barking, tugging on their leashes, sniffing one another's behinds; I counted four—Rex's classmates at Canine Connections. Like him, they were enrolled in a twelve-week training course to become service dogs. The instant I took stock of them, a flashback jingle popped into my head. *"One of these things is not like the others."*

Even a *Sesame Street*–watching toddler could figure this one out. The other dogs were young. The others were purebreds. The others had smooth, shiny coats, two alert ears, and well-behaved tails.

And then there was Rex, a big galumph of indeterminate age, with a stringy coat and unkempt tail working like a runaway dust mop. In a room full of best-in-shows, Rex was the poster boy for mutt-dom; nothin' but a pound dog.

"Don't worry, I won't let you down, Lacey." Yes, I was still hearing him talk. Yes, he seemed to mangle my name every time. So no, a return to sanity didn't seem likely right then.

Here's what I know about service dogs: Blind people use them to help cross the street. Police employ K9 units to sniff out drugs and land mines. Hero dogs find missing children and long-buried bodies.

I get it. Canine training is commendable, but so is housing the homeless, feeding the hungry, finding a cure for incurable diseases, or saving wildlife from oil spills. The point is, causes and the do-gooders who do them are totally worthy. Once, I *was* them. Just not now.

I checked the time. In exactly ninety minutes, I'd better be in my room with the door closed. For now, I was stuck in *this* room, long, low-ceilinged, rectangular. It looked like a grimy-windowed school gym, and smelled like a kennel. The aroma of "eau de dog" nearly choked me. I could get used to it, but Regan? Not so much.

The other kids had begun to settle on the folding chairs set up in a row. I took the end chair and pretended to pay attention to a toned, attractive woman with short neat hair who wore an oversize T-shirt. It had a picture of a big floppy-eared dog with a word bubble over his head. *"Hello! My name is 'No, no, bad dog.' What's yours?"*

Her name was actually LuLu. She would be our instructor. "Welcome to Canine Connections's Teen class, or what we refer to as Kids4Kids. As young people yourselves, you'll be training assistance dogs specifically meant for disabled children and young adults. Our goal is to help these kids—our recipients— gain greater independence and increase their quality of life."

"My dog will go to live with a child in a wheelchair?"

The girl who'd asked the question was around Regan's age with long black hair. She stroked the beautiful dark brown dog at her feet.

"Mainly," LuLu acknowledged, "but we train dogs for recipients with varied physical and mental disabilities, including muscular dystrophy, multiple sclerosis, cerebral palsy, spinal cord injuries, blindness and hearing impairments, and autism. Once we had a child who had to sleep with a respirator. Her parents were always worried the respirator might stop and they wouldn't hear it. We trained a dog to wake her parents if that ever happened."

"Did it?" asked a girl holding the leash of a yellow Labrador retriever.

LuLu nodded. "That dog saved the child's life. By

the end of this training program, the dogs you're foster-ing may one day do the same for others in need."

I stole a glance at Rex. Did he know he was only being fostered? That living with us wasn't permanent? Rex chose that moment to list toward me and rest his snout on my lap. My thigh muscle tightened involun-tarily.

"The one thing all the people we help have in common," LuLu told us, "is a drive to become more independent—and all of you who've come here today are already part of that, by giving your dogs a loving, secure environment, socializing them, and teaching them basic skills like 'sit,' 'come,' 'stay,' and 'heel.'"

My family had done none of those things.

Translation: Regan fudged Rex's application! I bet she'd said we'd had the dog for months, had properly trained him, arranged playdates, and made sure he spent time around other people.

"Now it's your turn," said LuLu warmly. "Please introduce yourselves and tell us why the four-legged friend you've brought will make a great service dog."

I flinched, and prayed to go last. Luckily, LuLu nod-ded at the girl with the long black hair sitting farthest from me.

"I'm Megan, and this is Romeo—he's a chocolate Labrador retriever." She ran her hand along his gleaming coat proudly and the dog responded by sitting upright and posing royally. "Romeo is more than a dog—he's an old soul and I think he was put on this earth to help others."

Was he put on earth to bring world peace, too? I wondered snarkily.

Sitting next to Romeo, the vanilla to his chocolate, was Daffodil, a pale yellow Lab who was two years old, and impeccably groomed. Her human companion was Maria. She and her mom had been fostering service dogs for years. "Once you meet the child your dog is going to, you're never the same," she said with a heavy Spanish accent. "You wonder why everyone doesn't do this. It's such a kindness."

Next up sat—or rather slouched—Lissa, whose jutting chin and folded arms made her look defiant and defensive. I wondered what her saga was.

"I have to be here, for community service." She practically spit out the word "community." "Otherwise, I go back to juvie. Which sucks worse than this."

LuLu didn't seem surprised. "And your dog?" she prompted.

Lissa's dog, a sable, black, and tan German shepherd, was sitting with his backside on her feet, until she kicked him off. "He belongs to Family Services. His name is Chainsaw."

How fitting.

"Do you know why the dog is sitting on your feet?" LuLu asked the girl.

"He's always up in my space," she complained.

"He's protecting you," LuLu explained. "You give off a vibe that something's wrong. The dog's instinct is to protect you. That's how he shows it."

Lissa scowled. "I don't need protection."

In direct contrast to insolent Lissa was the preppy-looking guy next to me, dressed in pressed khakis and a red Hilfiger shirt tucked into his belt. "Hello," he said smoothly. "I'm Trey, and this is Clark Kent—he comes from a long line of champions. Tiny but mighty!"

The dog looked like a multicolored Snausage, long and low to the ground. He had the shortest legs this side of a dachshund—and weirdly? No tail.

"He's a purebred blue merle Pembroke Welsh corgi," Trey bragged, though clearly that meant nothing to anyone in the room. "Nothing stops this guy. Clark Kent's going to make a *super*"—he paused so we could get the lame joke—"companion for the disabled."

I suddenly got it. Trey, who looked to be around seventeen, was probably doing the same thing as Regan: using the dog as a cause-related résumé-booster.

LuLu gave Trey a tight smile, and turned expectantly to me. I lifted my eyebrows and cleared my throat.

"Um, I'm Grace, and this is Rex." Rex raised his head and managed to get one ear to stand at attention. "I'm not sure what exact breed he is . . ." I trailed off. If the trainer was going to notice that Rex didn't exactly fit in with this exemplary lineup, now would be the moment to mention it.

"Is Rex a shelter dog?" LuLu came forward and knelt in front of Rex, inspecting him.

I nodded, almost hopeful. Could that eliminate him from the program?

"That's so wonderful!" declared LuLu, scratching a spot on Rex's head. "You rescued a dog, who'll now go on to improve someone else's life. That's what we call win-win."

So. Not. Getting. Kicked. Out.

"And why do you think Rex is ready to be trained as a service dog?" LuLu inquired.

Because my sister thinks it'll look good on her résumé, blared the thought bubble over my head.

"Tell her you're not sure yet," Rex advised me.

I blinked and stared at him. He'd tilted his head and looked at me expectantly. For a split second I imagined everyone had heard him. But no, all eyes in the room were on me.

"I . . . I'm not sure . . . yet," I stammered.

"That's an honest answer." LuLu laughed.

If dogs could crow, that's how I'd describe Rex's bewhiskered, beaming face.

"In fact, you all have great, admirable reasons—and on behalf of everyone at Canine Connections, we thank you for being here. But . . ." She paused, affecting a serious look. "I have to be honest. We'll work hard and do our best, but it's possible not all of your dogs will make it. They'll need to pass the Public Access Test to become certified."

I scanned the line of dogs and caught myself thinking: Okay, so they're all purebreds, alert, dignified, and bright. But can they talk?

LuLu consulted her chart and furrowed her brow. "I think we're missing someone. Does anyone know where Otis is? He's a standard poodle, who's also signed up for this class. He's being fostered by a . . . Mr. . . ." She paused. "I can't make out the last name. It looks like Deco?"

No one seemed to know anything about the missing Otis or his owner.

LuLu got the class started. "Each week, we're going to work on a skill. Your dogs will learn to open and close doors, flick light switches, push elevator buttons, retrieve anything you ask—including his own leash and the remote control—shop for groceries, pay the cashier, even help a person in a wheelchair pop a curb."

A chorus of "No way" and "Really? How?" greeted LuLu's assertation.

I eyed Rex. *Bet he aces this baby.* I had no real reason to think so, but I did, strongly.

"We'll start with basics. Please choose a workstation, bring it to the center of the room, and let's teach your dog to jump up on it and 'stay' on command." By workstation, she was referring to three-foot square blocks of wood, the kind you see dogs posing on at dog shows.

"Keep your dogs on leashes at all times during training," LuLu advised—just as Trey was unhooking Clark Kent, who made a beeline for Daffodil, the yellow Lab. For her part, she seemed more interested in Romeo, the chocolate Lab, and proceeded to sniff his hind quarters. Romeo rolled over, submissive.

Cries of "Romeo—no!" and "Daffodil, come!" and "Clark Kent, stop that!" echoed through the cavernous space. Meanwhile, Rex and I dutifully followed directions. I chose the least scratched-up block and dragged it into the center of the room. Rex raised his head, looking at me as if waiting for a command. "Up, Rex!" I said, patting the block, feeling confident.

The dog didn't move a muscle.

"Rex, you're supposed to jump up here." I indicated the top of the block again. Stubbornly, Rex remained sitting by my feet. Three more times I showed him what to do; three more times he pretended not to understand.

By now, all the other dogs were atop their blocks—although it'd taken dwarf-legged Clark Kent several tries. At the risk of looking lame and feeling really stupid—I didn't want to be the only one whose dog wouldn't follow the first, simplest command—I stooped to his level. That is, I bent down to *talk* to him. I felt ridiculous whispering, "What's wrong? Why aren't you jumping up?"

"What's in it for me?" he whispered back.

Before I got a chance to react, LuLu came to the rescue.

"We don't always reward our dogs with snacks," she said, handing out Baggies filled with Pup-Peroni training bits. "But since this is the first time, we're going to give them treats for following instructions."

Rex grinned. I gave him the stink-eye.

The rest of the class flew by. We worked on eye contact with our dogs, and the command "stay." We walked several feet away, and then instructed the dogs to "come."

Once he was sure a treat was on the other end, Rex was a model student. Which I couldn't say for Romeo, who spent most of the time on his back, and Clark Kent, who, once up, refused to leave his block.

Just before the end of class, LuLu gave us each a zippered nylon pouch.

"Goodie bags!" raved Rex, his tail wagging like a windshield wiper on high speed. "I hope there are chicken strips! Or rawhide chews!"

"Inside are the vests we call capes," LuLu explained. "Whenever your dog is on a leash—indoors or out— they must wear it. I'll demonstrate how to put them on." She motioned at Rex. "Would you like to be my helper?"

Obediently, Rex trotted forward.

The capes were bright green and fit like a harness across his chest and back, over his flanks, and fastened underneath. On top, the warning DON'T PET! stood out in black lettering. On each side, reflective strips were affixed to pockets, like doggy-sized saddlebags, with SERVICE DOG IN TRAINING clearly visible.

I looked at the cape. I looked at Rex. This wasn't going to be attractive. Then I thought of my fashionista sister, with visions of a snowy white fluffball accessorized like a sparkling Barbie-dog. We were stuck with a cape-clad doofus-dog instead. The urge to laugh hit me—so strange that I nearly choked.

And then my heart stopped.

The door flew open, and a boy in shabby lowriders and a hoodie that obscured his face blasted into the

room—incongruously dragging a large snow-white poodle. He headed for LuLu. "Sorry, man, I know I'm late.
My ride never showed."

A cold gust of wind blew across my heart. The voice
was unmistakable. It belonged to someone I'd sworn
never to set eyes on again.

· · 5 · ·

At Risk

What was that about?" Rex demanded, screeching to a stop on the sidewalk. He was miffed that I'd abruptly yanked him out of class. "I was going to be her helper. Helpers get snacks."

"We're going home," I snapped.

"How?" Rex asked, looking around. "I don't see a ride."

"We'll walk," I said, so rattled that I no longer cared about being insane for hearing him—let alone answering. I stomped off.

Stubbornly, Rex stayed put. No amount of tugging the leash could move him. I dropped it on the ground and kept walking.

"Please, Tracey, tell me about it," Rex begged, reluctantly trotting after me, dragging his leash along the sidewalk. "I'm an excellent listener."

"How's that possible when you're always talking?" I

retorted, then immediately felt a stab of guilt. Same as I'd had in the kennel, when Regan said, right in front of him, that he wasn't cute. I didn't want to hurt his feelings. Maybe that's why I continued to talk to him.

"Not that it's any of your business, but that subhuman with the poodle who just blew into class? He belongs behind bars."

"Is this about your dad?"

"What? What did you say?" Stunned, I whipped around and shot daggers at Rex. How could the dog know? I mean, he obviously can't really be talking . . . so how is it I heard him make a connection between that gang-hanger-on and my dad?

"You don't know what you're talking about!" I said, storming off again.

Two kids on skateboards stopped short to stare. One twirled his forefinger by his ear, the universal sign for "nutso."

Rex ignored them and turned back to me. "Hey, a dog learns things, living with someone. Wanna talk about it?"

"No! I do not want to talk about it." I kept walking.

We'd gotten only a few blocks from Canine Connections when Regan pulled up. Noting the fury on my face and the force I used slamming the door, Einstein guessed, "Bad session?"

"Why don't *you* tell her?" I directed my question at the four-legged backseat blabbermouth.

Regan arched a perfectly shaped eyebrow and emitted a low whistle. "Okaaay, I guess I got my answer."

"You didn't even get the question," I snapped. "I'll break it down: I'm not going back there. So if you want a certified service dog, you better clear your oh-so-busy schedule."

"Okay," she said lightly as she hit the gas and made a sharp left turn into a busy intersection. In other circumstances, I would have screamed, adding my terrified indignation to the screeching tires, blaring of horns, and swear words being thrown at her.

Instead, I spent the rest of the drive staring out the side window, trying not to think.

∾

Shockingly, Regan did take Rex to his next class.

Predictably, she ended up in my room right afterward.

I knew exactly why.

I turned the volume up on my iPod. Bruce Springsteen, the Boss, as Dad called him, was rasping out "Born to Run." Blithely, Regan arranged her long limbs on the end of my bed and pinned me with her baby-blue anime eyes. "They asked for you at Canine Connections," she began. "They really like you—they say you're a natural with the dogs."

Flattery? Really? Surely she can do better than that.

I started to sing really loudly, "Tramps like us! Baby we were born to run! Uh-oh-oh! Oh-oh-oh-oh, ooo . . . !"

Regan tried again: "I totally get why you don't want to go back."

I muted Bruce.

"It's a hard class," she whined. "They don't let you text or take any breaks. And the smell in that room—pee-*yeew!*"

I turned the volume back up. The Boss had ceded to Bon Jovi and I sang out, "Oh! Oh! We're halfway there. Oh! Oh! Livin' on a prayer . . ."

"It's because of that boy, isn't it? He's the reason you don't want to go back."

My jaw dropped and I killed the music. It took her only three tries?

But then she blew it. "He's so obnoxious! And his little dog with those gross stunted legs kept nipping at my ankles."

I started to say "the other boy, you moron," but something got caught in my throat and I ended up making a cackling noise. It didn't matter. If Regan didn't know—and why would she, denier that she is?—there wasn't anything I could do to change her.

She wasn't the one who begged Mom to let her go with her to Dad's precinct, who sat behind the one-way mirrored glass when the police questioned suspects.

On November 22 of last year, Police Detective Gregory Abernathy—my dad—was leaving work when someone shot him from a speeding car. There were no eyewitnesses. The surveillance camera caught part of a license plate, and a grainy picture of the back of four heads in that car.

Experts determined that whoever shot my dad had been sitting in the front seat—most likely the driver—and was most definitely right-handed. They found the car's owner, nineteen-year-old Hector Lowe. He was no stranger to the police. A suspected gang member, Hector had a rap sheet a mile long. They brought him and his thug buddies in for questioning. They all claimed to know nothing about a shooting.

Liars.

At that point, the police didn't know if the shooting was a random drive-by, or the handiwork of someone who knew my dad, possibly even one of the at-risk kids he worked with. These were foster kids, neglected kids, abused kids, the kind I should feel sorry for but am mainly scared of—the kids who are bound for juvie, the Palm Beach County Juvenile Correctional Facility.

Mom didn't want me there. The police *really* didn't want me there. I talked my way in by saying I might recognize one of them, from school or something. But that wasn't my real reason for insisting on witnessing the questioning.

I thought I would know, just by their faces, their voices, their body language, and more than anything, their eyes—which one of these monsters had cut down a truly good man, a giving and funny and caring teddy bear of a man. I was his daughter, the one who thought his lame jokes were funny, who played catch with him, who got into raptor-rock like Bruce Springsteen and Bon Jovi because of him, the one whose softball team he coached. The one whose fault it was that he left work early that day and stepped into the line of fire.

I should have been able to pinpoint the perp.

But I didn't know. All I remember is a revolving door of sullen faces, belligerent denials, feigned ignorance. My dad had tried to improve their lives. Any one of them could have ended his.

Even Joey Pico—JJ to his posse. Even though he proved to be left-handed, he was the only one who admitted to being in the car that day.

That was enough for me. If he didn't do it himself, he knew who did. The police couldn't get anything more out of him. They had no solid reason to hold him. I'd been so disgusted, I'd sworn to never set eyes on him again.

Joey Pico was the kid who'd blown through the door at Canine Connections.

··6··

What the Dog Heard

Of course I went back. I knew as well as Regan did that eventually I'd give in. The sad truth is that when it comes to my sister, I've folded so many times I'm surprised I don't see an origami swan when I look in the mirror.

I put up a good fight, though. I took my case to Mom, explaining that I didn't want to be on the same planet, let alone in the same room, with one of the goons involved in Dad's death. I was sure Mom would be horrified, shocked at the turn of events.

So wrong.

She wasn't shocked at all that a known felon— well, okay, maybe not an actual felon, but a suspected one—was in the same Canine Connections class as the victim's daughter. Me.

Mom mused, "I wonder if that boy is in the East Coast Assistance Dogs program—they work with Canine Connections."

The what?

"They choose specific at-risk teens to train service dogs," Mom explained. "It's supposed to allow kids who've been abandoned or abused to receive unconditional love from these dogs, and learn responsibility, discipline, and empathy for someone who has it worse than they do."

I flashed on Lissa. She had to be part of that program, too. It was her community service to keep her out of juvie.

As if I cared about the East Coast whatever program.

Then Mom dropped the D-bomb. Dad.

"Your dad was a big fan of ECAD, you know. He saw good results with the kids he worked with—saw it boost their self-esteem, made them more compassionate toward other people, less likely to turn to violence."

Bringing Dad into it was low. Before I could tell her what I thought of that, she made it worse: "It's even possible that Dad recommended this boy, JJ, for the program."

Come *on*, did I really need to remind her that this boy was a suspect?

As if she could read my mind, Mom said, "He *was* under suspicion, honey. They ruled him out."

They gave up, is what I wanted to say. I scowled.

My mom reached out to touch my hand; instinctively, I pulled it away. "Please don't say I have to let it go, okay?"

"I understand if you don't want to be in that class, and I'll support you. Tell Regan she's got to do it herself."

I would have. Except for Rex, who'd been on my case ever since the one class with Regan. "Please, Jacey, oh, please!" Rex kept up his whining. "It's no fun going with Regan—she's not like you. She doesn't even pay attention!"

Bizarrely, Rex's talking was starting to seem—I can't believe I'm saying it—normal. Maybe it was just easier to go along with this weirdness than to keep trying to convince myself it was all in my head. Because if that were true, it was time for the men in the white suits to come and take me away.

"I'll protect you from him—from that boy you don't like," Rex asserted. As if to prove it, Rex sat upright, puffed his wiry chest out in his version of a guard-dog pose. But with his chaotically colored prickly hair sticking out in all directions, one ear upright, the other folded down, he hardly looked like he could guard a parakeet.

But there it was, a little ice cap melted inside me . . .

. . . and, strangely, re-formed into an idea.

No, not an idea. A thought. A thread of a thought, which, over the next several hours wound itself into a possibility.

What if I could pull off what the cops couldn't? What if, somehow during those class hours—maybe even with Rex's help—I could wear JJ Pico down, or trick him into telling the truth about what really happened that day?

It wasn't going to be easy. I may be a nutcase for hearing a dog talk, but I'm not delusional.

And I know nothing can bring my dad back. Just like nothing can change the fact that it was all my fault.

If I hadn't guilted him into leaving work early that day, he wouldn't have been out there when that car drove by. Maybe no one would have gotten shot. But I wanted him there for my after-school softball tryouts. Originally, he'd begged off coming; he was slammed at work. But his workload was no match for my petty selfishness. I wanted to show off, see him cheering for me when I made the team ('cause I was sure I would). I wouldn't take no for an answer and pulled a Regan. I pouted and pretty-pleased until I wore him down. So he left early, intending to come see me play. And walked right into a drive-by.

If I hadn't been so selfish, he might still be alive.

There was no way to tell him how sorry I was, but maybe I could do this one thing: get justice for him.

❧

Uplifted by my newfound hope, I tried to think of a way to get JJ to tell me what he hadn't told the police. There were several obstacles to that goal.

The biggest? I hated him. The *idea* of getting him to talk was one thing. Doing it meant being close enough for a conversation, and that turned my stomach.

Unless there was another way.

One thing I knew about bad guys—or any guys who think they got away with something—is they like to brag. Especially to someone they want to impress. Someone who'd give him props for committing a crime and getting away with it.

Someone like Lissa.

She'd made it clear that her only reason for being in Canine Connections was to avoid juvie. She and JJ had at least that in common. And sure enough, the delinquent duo had formed their little Future Felons of America club. In class, they were always together.

Normally, I would have stayed as far away from them as I could in the gymnasium-sized room. Now I had to get closer. For a week and a half, Rex and I chose workstations that inched us nearer to them. All I needed was to accidentally-on-purpose overhear JJ brag about his exploits. I'd have something the police did not. My secret weapon? Rex. What I couldn't hear, he could—especially if they were whispering.

All dogs have supersonic hearing. My dog can tell me what he heard. Better, Rex was totally into playing detective.

"That's a great idea, Spacey! I'm all over it."

For the first few days, Rex's reports were disappointing—unless it was Lissa I wanted to snare. The only time she talked animatedly was to brag about fights she'd gotten into, cigarettes she'd cribbed, stores she'd ripped off. JJ didn't seem to have any problem with any of this. But if he was matching or one-upping her with tales of his own unlawful actions, neither Rex nor I ever heard it.

Finally, after nearly two weeks of semi-stalking, we got a sort-of break. Rex did, that is.

"Lissa's planning to rob someone's house!" he told me excitedly. "She's got it all cased out."

"Not cool," I agreed. "But how does that help us nail JJ?"

"She wants him in on it."

What the Dog Saw

One Friday, Mom, not Regan, picked me and Rex up after class. Which was unusual by itself, more so that she was wearing cute white capris and strappy sandals, instead of her standard "teacher-wear"—long flowy skirt, blousy top with a matching string of beads, and flats.

"I'm going to my widow's support group, and afterward, we're all having dinner at the Ocean Grill. It's for someone's birthday. They say," she said, like she was still convincing herself, "you're supposed to celebrate the good times."

"Have a good time," I said, wondering what, if anything, Mom got out of her bereavement support group meetings. "Tell whoever I said happy birthday."

Too late, I realized my mistake. Mom took my

comment to mean I was in a talkative, receptive mood, and launched into the dreaded subject . . .

"Speaking of having a good time . . ." She was off and running. About how I haven't spent any time with my friends, haven't gone out, even though she knows—because she bumped into Jasmine's mom—that my friends have been trying to coax me out of my shell. "Mrs. Richards mentioned a barbecue tonight at Kendra's house—"

I cut her off. "I know you think it's best for me, Mom, and I will . . . join them again. Not today though."

"When?" She kept her gaze on the road steady.

"Soon."

"Your mom is right, Stacie. You should go—and bring me! I'm all about barbecues and pool parties!"

Et tu, Brute? I nearly blurted, though I was getting much better at not addressing Rex in the presence of others. I did put some value on my sanity, or the pretense of it.

Mom still hadn't exhausted the topic, when, fifteen minutes later, she dropped me at home. "Regan has some friends over. Maybe you want to call Mercy or Jasmine and join them?"

I jumped out of the car without answering. As Mom carefully backed out of our narrow driveway, her face fell just a bit: she knew I wouldn't do it. "I miss your smile, Grace," she said as she pulled onto Abacoa Drive.

"I'll be fine, Mom," I called after her. "Stop worrying."

I opened our front door to a wall of noise. Dance-club music, my least favorite, bounced off the walls, accented with the jokey, knowing, upbeat voices of Regan's friends, male and female. Worse than bad music was the sound of laughter. It felt like an assault on my ears, like the eardrum-piercing squeal of an out-of-sync microphone.

"Weiners!" Rex exclaimed, eyes shining, tongue hanging out. "I smell pigs in blankets!!"

Food plus dance music plus guys: this wasn't having a couple of friends over. Regan was having a party! Who does that when their father died just six months ago? Well, five months and fourteen days ago.

The last thing I wanted was to be suckered into joining them. I had to slip by unnoticed. But all the rooms in my one-level house are off a main hallway—it's hard to avoid being seen. Not that I wasn't going to try.

Hoping the house music would cover up Rex's nails making clickity-clack sounds on the hallway floor, I snuck a glance into the living room. I counted seven of Regan's friends: bestie Sheena, Sheena's boyfriend, Regan's current boy-lapdog, plus four random Regan-wannabes. They were scattered around the coffee table, lounging on the couch, perched on armchairs, flopped out on the floor, using our fringed throw pillows as backrests.

I'd made it well past the archway of the living room when I gave myself away. It wasn't the inane conversation that unhinged me:

"You're a lock for PSD, Regan," said Lapdog. "A slam dunk."

"What's a PSD?" one of the morons asked. "Is that like PMS, or some syndrome?"

Regan clarified, "It's Parsons School of Design. It's actually called Parsons: The New School for Design. It's the best school for fashion and design. I've got my heart set on it."

"You're so talented," gushed someone else. "You'll totally make it."

"I hope so. I pulled decent grades, and I think my portfolio of fashions is pretty good, but I tanked on my PSATS. My first try at the SATS weren't much better," Regan replied ruefully.

"College is over a year away, why are you so obsessed with it?" That voice I recognized as Sheena's.

"I'm not obsessed, I'm planning," Regan corrected her.

"You do have that ace in the hole," Sheena's boyfriend commented. "Wish I'd thought of it—who trains service dogs? It's such a gimme. The essay part of your application is going to rock."

"Already got it started," Regan said proudly.

She did? She'd been to *one* class. I'd been going for weeks. I shook my head in disbelief.

But none of that "all-hail Regan" banter was what freaked me out.

This did, courtesy of Sheena: "It doesn't matter what you write, or how good your fashions are. Just play the daddy-death card. That's like an all-access pass to college."

I about-faced, stormed into party central, and glared at Regan. "It isn't bad enough you're having a party—now Dad's a *card*?"

"Grace! You scared me!" Regan scolded. Her hand flew to her chest. "Don't do that again."

I stood there with my hands on my hips, too infuriated to know what else to say.

"And as for having a few friends over," Regan countered, "you should try it."

I'm sure I was the only one who noticed the slight waver in her voice. It was enough to mollify me. Almost.

Still, I needed to get out of there, dignity intact. "Since you all seem so interested," I said, practically shoving poor Rex in front of me, "here's the dog *Regan's* trained so well. Notice his fashionable service dog vest. Do a trick, Rex."

I pivoted, dashed down the hall, and slammed my door.

❧

The trick Rex performed was for me. I don't know how much time had gone by, but I suddenly became aware of something ramming against my door. I knew that sound. In class, Rex had learned to open doors by following the commands "Up!" and "Tug!"

Rex must have gotten up on his hind legs, grabbed the rope I'd hung on the handle for practicing, and tugged the door open. I half expected some self-congratulatory babble, but Rex was superserious. His tail pointed downward.

"Come with me," he said. "You have to see something."

"Not going back out there," I told him.

"Me neither! The hors d'oeuvres are gone, that greedy kid ate the Whole Foods' gluten-free mini-bagels and lox without even offering me any. Some people are so rude."

Not in the mood for Rex's snack obsession, I brushed him off. "If you have to go outside, take yourself—you can clearly open the door. Just be sure to close it on the way out."

"It's not that," he said in a tone so hushed it made me nervous.

"If you're here to nag me about my homework, don't."

"We have to go to your mom's room."

"Why?"

"Follow me," Rex said. "Please, Pacey."

Whatever. I slid off the bed.

Feeling stupid, I followed Rex to the end of the hall. The door was closed, and there was no rope hanging on the end of the handle. But unlike the circular doorknob I have, Mom's had a lever handle. Rex swatted at it. A giant hairy paw came down hard on the lever. The door flew open.

My parents' bedroom. I was having trouble getting used to it as Mom's room, even though the nightstand on Dad's side of the bed was empty, while Mom's was piled high with books about what happens when your husband dies, like *The Year of Magical Thinking* and *Widow*.

I half expected to see *Widowhood for Dummies*, but apparently no one had thought of that yet.

I didn't expect to see Sheena Weston, frozen like an ice carving in front of the bureau. Mom's jewelry box was open, and Regan's best friend was holding up a necklace, as if pondering a purchase. Only she looked less like a fashion fabulista than a frightened ferret caught in the klieg lights.

"What are you doing?" I asked, utterly confused.

"Nothing." She shrugged casually. "I mean . . . I was looking for the bathroom."

"You've been in this house a hundred times. The bathroom hasn't moved."

She forced a laugh. "Well, duh. No, I mean I got up to go, and Regan asked me to get a necklace—she wants to see how it goes with her new outfit."

What part of that made no sense? All of it.

Rex growled low. "Tell her to give you her bag."

Sensing something, Sheena protectively pinned her bulky shoulder bag close to her body.

"You're stealing from us?" The words felt ridiculous coming out of my mouth.

Without warning, Rex rocketed toward her, snatched the bag in his jaw, and shook his head frantically. Amid Sheena's wails of protest, the bag fell open. On the floor mixed in with her wallet, lip gloss, and cell phone, I recognized Mom's diamond tennis bracelet, her gold locket necklace . . . and Dad's wedding ring.

I was reeling. The full-out meltdown I'd so far avoided was coming at me like an onrushing train. Rex saved me from myself. He barked wildly, while circling Sheena menacingly. One thing about an unkempt shelter dog: they do an excellent menacing.

"Get that dog away from me!" Sheena cringed. "He's going to bite me."

"He won't, but I will," I threatened. "I'm going to tell Regan."

Sheena's face registered *real* fear. With two hands, she hastily grabbed her bag, wallet, cell phone, and lip gloss. Then she ran.

"You'll never hog hors d'ouevres in this house again!" Rex said to Sheena's fleeing back.

I knelt and put my arms around the mangy mutt,

whose coat felt porcupine-prickly, but warm and sooth-
ing all the same. "Rex, how did you know she was
stealing? Please don't tell me you can see through walls."

"I smelled something fishy going on," he said. "I
thought it was lox."

My chest heaved as if trying for a laugh, but a raw
rasp came out instead. My mom would have been dev-
astated to lose Dad's wedding ring.

Gently, I picked up Mom's jewelry. I closed my fist
around the simple gold ring and debated what to do. The
thought of busting Sheena in front of her friends was
enticing, but I doubted the she-thief had stuck around.
For a fleeting second, I pictured myself marching into
the living room and announcing the betrayal. Minus a
surveillance tape—let alone Rex as my only witness—
I'd probably be laughed out of the room.

Or worse. My sister might believe me. I couldn't
hurt Regan like that. Not in front of everyone.

In the end, I decided to leave the nearly stolen necklace in her room, and I hoped she'd ask me about it.
Whatever she'd do, it'd be in private.

The first thing I noticed when I walked into Regan's
room was her laptop. It was open to a document. <u>Appli-
cation for Parsons: The New School for Design. Writing
Sample.</u>

The essay!

Was there any way I wasn't going to read it? Even in light of what'd just happened, I wasn't that distracted. Applicants had to choose from three topics:

1. Evaluate a significant experience, achievement, risk you have taken, or ethical dilemma you have faced and its impact upon you.
2. Discuss some issue of personal, national, or international concern and its importance to you.
3. Indicate a person who has had a significant influence on you, and describe that influence.

Predictably, Regan had gone for #1, "A Significant Achievement," by Regan Abernathy.

This semester, I decided to rescue a dog from a shelter and then train it to help a disabled person. I knew it wasn't going to be an easy task, but I felt I was up to it. My dog's name is Rex. While he isn't a purebred, he is really smart. (And cute.) I took him to classes three times a week, at Canine Connections, where he learned how to help an unbalanced person, like someone who might have cerebral palsy or another

disease, have better balance. He can lead
a blind person, open doors for people in
wheelchairs, turn on and off light switches,
and press the button for the elevator.
He can even give the cashier your credit
card after you make a purchase. In fact,
my dog knows eighty commands! Rex is going
to be an awesome service dog! And service
dogs make people's lives better. Below I
have designed some original accessories
so my dog will be fashionable as well as
functional.

Here, Regan had sketched doggy Uggs, studded col-
lars, leashes adorned with sequins, and even a neon-
pink sweater.

Two impulses pulled at me. I wanted to highlight
the whole essay and hit delete.

But I also wanted to fix it.

·· 8 ··

Not Forgetting

Like any school in Anytown, USA, Jupiter Middle School has its cliques: the gods and goddesses, the gearheads, geeks, goths, and the going-straight-to-juvies. Then there's the one most people belong to, the "get-bys"—the non-standouts, the under-the-radars who don't merit the spotlight, but aren't lame enough to be losers.

I was a get-by.

I was content. The spotlight was never my best light.

Everything changed when I returned to school in the beginning of December. I was no longer Grace Abernathy: get-by. I was "the girl whose dad got killed." A celebrity.

The goddess-girls, who'd never noticed me before, pretended to be close personal friends. They'd sidle up, squeeze my arm, and say something syrupy like, "I heard what happened. Sorry," accompanied by a phony sympathetic look. A few said that if I wanted to hang out—or sit with them at lunch—that would be cool.

As if I *wanted* to be popular-by-tragedy.

They pitied me. I loathed them.

On the flip side, some kids I'd been friendly with acted as if I had the plague. They avoided me completely, even averted their eyes when I was around. Like losing your dad was contagious.

The few who made it easy didn't overthink it. They just blurted out in passing, "Yo, heard your old man got shot by a gang—sucks, dude," and kept on walking. No reaction required.

Most offensive were the leaders of the God Squad, Meredith Hess and Teresa Gomez, who tried to make me their special project, offering to accompany me to teen survivors' groups, giving me Bibles and books, forwarding posts I should read, links I should click on. *The Dead Father's Club*, really? As if befriending me gave them points with the Almighty or something. I admit I was just waiting for them to say, "It's all part of God's plan." Or "It'll make you stronger." Or "He's in a better place."

Because if they had? I'm a peaceful person, but I might've gone all Pat Tillman's brother on them. Pat Tillman was the war hero whose death by friendly fire was covered up by the military. At his funeral, famous people said things like, "He's in a better place now." And Pat Tillman's brother got up and, um—angrily disagreed.

The varied reactions of my peers—"God," bad, and ugly—paled in comparison to the worst person of all, Ms. Downy—Downer, or Dowdy, kids call her behind her back—the school-appointed grief counselor. At first, I pictured her like an arts and crafts counselor, only for grief issues. I thought she might have me make a collage depicting my feelings.

What she did was way worse. She told me she knew "exactly how I felt."

Really? She knows how it feels to not be able to breathe because every breath feels like a knife to the lungs? How a cold emptiness can take up as much room inside you as multiple pig-outs? Unless she was me, she couldn't know.

I couldn't forget . . .

It was just after last period and I was on the athletic field along with Jazz, Kendra, Mercy, and several dozen girls trying out for the middle school's junior varsity softball team. I remember the sharp tingly smell of just-mowed grass and the crunching sound my cleats made as I crossed the field. I ran my hand over the raised gold stitching of my softball jersey spelling out WARRIORS, and the number—my number if I made the team—22, also stitched in gold on our blue-and-white uniform. My striped knee-highs met the hem of my white softball pants and itched just below the kneecap. My hair was a little short to be pulled back into a proper ponytail, but I thought it'd look cool if I gathered it and threaded it through the back of my softball cap.

It was November, a perfect time of the year where I live, warm and breezy, with not much humidity. The palm trees around the field tickled the sky. But my eyes kept returning to the bleachers. Five rows up, east-facing, between home plate and first base, that's where my dad would be sitting.

Dad would normally be at work that time of day. But I'd coaxed him into leaving early.

Other parents were there, mostly moms, but so far, there'd been no sign of Dad. Didn't matter. The positions I'd tried out for so far—outfield, shortstop, first base, pitcher—were not my position.

Catcher. That was me.

A position my body type—short, compact, and strong—is uniquely suited for. Not to brag, but I have a precise eye, and I'm a really good catcher. Now, watching others try out for the position, I knew it was in the bag.

I just needed my dad to be there when my turn came up.

When it did, twenty minutes later, he still wasn't

there, but unless I was hallucinating, my mom was crossing the field. Mom rarely came to games, and never to tryouts. She was wearing her teacher clothes, today a long saffron skirt and matching blousy top. Sensible flats.

Crouched at home plate, I raised my glove up to pocket the ball being pitched by Jasmine. Jazz is a lousy pitcher, so I was more focused on how far away the ball was going to fly than wondering about my mom materializing. But as she got closer, I saw her face clearly. It was blotchy, as if she'd broken out in hives, and streaked with mascara lines. She was saying something to the first base coach, who promptly signaled for a time-out.

This was making no sense at all.

I felt a tap on the shoulder, so I stood up and swiveled around. Regan was here, too? Big sunglasses covered her face—but I could tell she was neither smirking, posing, or pouting, her usual repertoire of expressions. And to my shame, I remember thinking: Mom and Regan are here. I must've already been picked for JV and they're here for a surprise celebration. That was my last coherent thought before my memory shatters into kaleidoscopic slivers of glass.

Coach ordered the field cleared. When Mom reached me, she said nothing at first, just cradled me in her arms. I was so embarrassed! All eyes were fixed on me as the girls, headed for the lockers, filed past. I should have realized a whole lot sooner that Mom would never hug me like that in front of other people.

Unless she couldn't stop herself.

Smoothing my pitiful little stub of a ponytail, she sobbed into my ear, "Oh baby, we need to go now."

I have no memory of getting into our car. I was surprised that someone else—a police officer—was driving. Fast. Weaving in and out of traffic, down Military Trail, onto Route 95, off at the 45th Street exit. A siren blared, obscuring my hearing. That's probably why I didn't hear my mom trying to explain what had happened. I think my teeth were chattering.

We pulled up to St. Mary's Medical Center. I'd only ever been there once before, when a line drive hit Kendra in the head and she had a concussion. I remember the hospital lobby being spacious, airy, and antiseptic smelling, but today all I could see were dust motes floating inside streaks of sunlight.

We were hustled into an elevator, then guided along one corridor and turned down another corridor, maze-like. My cleats squeaked on the polished linoleum floor. I wondered if that was breaking some kind of "no cleats" rule, like they have at the library.

I'm ashamed to say, even standing with my mom and Regan outside his room, a nondescript cubicle in a busy intensive care unit with only a thin muslin curtain shrouding his bed, my brain still could not, or stubbornly would not, connect the dots.

I registered the presence of a stream of nurses passing by, walking around us as if we formed a boulder in a rushing river. A trio of scrubs-wearing doctors stood nearby, consulting among themselves in hushed tones. Beeping noises coming from behind the curtain kept a chaotic beat.

Mom was trying to talk to me, but she wasn't making any sense since she kept choking on her sobs.

Maybe that's why, in the end, all I heard was my sister's voice.

"Grace, you have to listen. Dad got shot while he was getting into his car. No one knows who shot him. He's not gonna make it, honey."

It's okay. It's okay. That's what I thought. No big if he doesn't make my tryouts.

"Does she want to see him?" One of the doctors, an intense guy with eyes as black as coal, had come up to us. He meant me. Did I want to see him? As if my mom and Regan already had.

Of course, I thought. I reached out to part the curtain that separated me from my dad.

Regan grabbed my shoulders and pulled me back. My big sister draped herself over me and whispered, "I don't think it's a good idea."

"She should say good-bye if she wants," my mom choked out, trembling. "Do you want to say good-bye, Gracie?"

Say good night, Gracie. That's what my father used to tell me every night before I headed off to bed. He said it was a joke from a classic TV show about a man with a ditzy wife named Gracie. At the close of every show, he'd tell her to address the audience and "Say good night, Gracie."

With a big, naive smile, she'd look directly at the audience and go, "Good night, Gracie."

Good night. Not good-bye.

"Good night, Gracie," I said numbly.

When Regan, my too-cool-for-the-room sister, wept, that's when the horror of what was happening began to sink in. I got it. And I lost it. I gulped great gobs of air. I hyperventilated until everything went white.

∾

"Hey, girl, figured I'd find you here." Mercy's voice snapped me back to the present. It was lunch period, and instead of hanging with my friends like I used to, these days I trek across the athletic field and plant myself in the bleachers. A familiar feeling of despair was settling over me today. My "big idea" about JJ was turning into a bust. We hadn't learned anything else about the potential robbery, and every time I forced myself near enough to say something, he turned away. It almost felt like he was repulsed by me, instead of the other way around. Like *he'd* been some sort of victim, and I was the perp.

Mercy climbed the benches and plopped down next to me. She looked cute with her hair in dreadlocks. Her nose ring glinted in the sun.

"Hey, Merce," I said, not unhappy to see her. "Bored of the cafeteria scene?"

"Not yet." Of my friends, Mercy knows me best. No way was she here to coax me inside, or do any version of the "it's time to get back to normal" dance.

"Social studies is next period," Mercy said, pulling a notebook out of her backpack. "And if . . . just in case you didn't do the homework . . . ?" She paused, though she'd guessed correctly.

". . . here." She opened her notebook and took out a neatly typed copy of the assignment in our World Cultures unit, "How geography has affected China's population distribution, economy, and culture."

My shoulders went slack. "Thanks, Merce. That's so cool." It really was, since Mercy had no mercy when Jazz cheated on a test. Now she was offering something almost as bad. "It's no big," I told her, turning down her offer. "I'll deal."

We spent the rest of the period together. I tore off bits of my egg salad sandwich and tossed them to some very excited seagulls. Mercy tried to entice them with her lunch—whatever organic concoction her health-nut mom had packed that day—but even seagulls, it seems, have their standards. Which did drag a giggle out of me.

I actually shocked myself by asking about the eighth-grade dance—not that I was going, but Mercy was on the committee.

"It's going good," she said. "I talked Rico Martinez into deejaying—"

"That's amazing!" I cut in. Rico's in high school and hands down the best spinner around. Getting him was a real coup.

Mercy beamed. She stopped short of asking if I would come. She knows better. When the bell rang signaling the end of the period, she did offer up her homework again. But I couldn't take it.

Whether I would have finagled my way out of yet another missed assignment or taken the F as Mr. Defendorf would likely give me—I'd reached my quota of incompletes in this class—I'll never know, because I got intercepted in the hallway by Mrs. Downy.

I frowned. Thought I was done with her.

"Hello, Grace. Would you mind following me to my office?"

I would mind very much, but doubted I had a choice.

"I've signed you out of social studies," she informed me. "Mr. Defendorf has excused you from this class."

"Guess I'll see you next period," I said to Mercy with a shrug.

"I'll take notes for you," she offered, and squeezed my shoulder in solidarity.

Mrs. Downy shut the door before taking her seat behind her gunmetal-gray desk. She clasped her hands and leaned forward, staring at me from behind her owl glasses, which only accentuated the deep pockets under her eyes. "How are you doing, Grace?"

I squirmed. *How do you think I'm doing?* is what I wanted to say, but I squashed my sarcasm. "Okay, I guess."

"While I'm not sure I agree with you, unfortunately, this is not a talk-therapy session—"

I exhaled, relieved. The last time I'd had to sit through her talk therapy, there was all sorts of psycho-babble about my life having "a new normal." I wonder what she'd say if I told her that my "new normal" involves a talking dog, a thief masquerading as my sister's BFF, and an unconvicted felon in my face three days a week.

"—I'm afraid we have to discuss your grades," she was saying.

I tensed.

"I've been given copies of your work from your teachers," she went on. "It doesn't show much effort."

That's because I don't care about them, I didn't say.

"In fact, from midterms on, it looks as if you haven't turned in many homework assignments, nor passed any exams. Your grades are slipping."

Feeling like I had to say something, I went with, "Sorry."

"How can we work together to reverse this trend?" she asked. A variation on the "help me help you" theme. I wanted this session—this non-talk-therapy session—to end. Sooner would be better than later.

"I'll try harder."

That wasn't going to cut it. "Should we go through your classes one by one and work out a plan?" Her eyes were now on her computer screen, where my less-than-sterling grades were listed before her.

"That's not necessary," I said quickly.

"It doesn't look good, Grace. Too many incompletes, Fs, and Ds."

Tell me something I don't know, I thought miserably.
And she did.

"At this rate, you'll have to repeat eighth grade. Grace, you're not going to graduate."

·· 9 ··

How a Color-Blind Dog Knows to Stop at Red Lights

Ask me if I care," I dared Rex.

"Don't have to ask, I know you do," Rex replied.

It no longer felt strange that we were talking, but we were taking a risk by doing it during a training session. When Rex was chattering away, everyone else heard dog noises—barks, yelps, whines, a low growl sometimes. But a girl having a full-out conversation with a dog looks like what it is: crazy-time.

Our dogs were perched atop their workstation blocks while we affixed harnesses on them. The harnesses were fitted with high, rectangular handles like the ones used on rolling suitcases. This is so the dog can accompany a blind person or someone with balance issues. Fastening the leather straps wasn't easy, especially on a dog who's arguing with you.

"You don't know anything," I said, buckling a thick leather strap across his chest.

"Dogs know more than you think. We can sense our humans' feelings," Rex asserted. "You're terrified of flunking out."

"Am not," I insisted while fastening the strap beneath his stomach just a little too tightly.

"Hey! Couldja loosen that? A dog's tummy needs room to expand, especially when treats are in the offing."

"That gravy train is coming to an end," I informed him, loosening the buckle beneath his bristly belly. "Soon all you get is praise and affection when you follow commands."

"But I always perform better when munchies are involved. Besides, at my age, who cares about having six-bone abs?"

"Chowhound," I muttered.

"Feelings-denier," Rex retorted.

"It's so nice that you talk to your dog like he's human," LuLu, our instructor, commented, inspecting the harness to make sure it was secure.

"He's so *not*—human," I said, but more to Rex than her.

Today was a big day. We were going on a field trip to teach our dogs how to lead a blind person, stop at curbs, and to wait for the green traffic light before crossing. Which, since dogs are color-blind, was a puzzler.

We trooped to a quiet neighborhood so there was no danger of a dog rushing into fast-moving traffic—or a Regan-like driver, I hoped.

The first part of the exercise was tedious, but uncomplicated. Grasping the harness handles, we gave the command "forward" and led the dogs straight ahead. Each time the dog did it exactly right, didn't veer off course, we clicked a handheld castanet-like gadget. The drill was simple: the dog obeys the command exactly, we click, and a treat is delivered at the sound of the click.

Soon most of the dogs had to only hear the word "forward"—even as we were standing still—to respond properly. It's surprising how motivating a liver-flavored Treat-Um can be! I couldn't help wondering what kind of treat it would take to motivate me to deal with the school debacle. Only one I could think of. But that would require a life rewind, where what happened, hadn't.

Next was teaching the dogs to stop at the curb. As soon as their paws landed on an upgrade or elevation in the sidewalk—a curb—we'd say, "Wait." If the dog stopped, he/she heard a click, followed immediately by a treat. The pattern, "forward," "stay," click-and-treat, was repeated until the dog did it right every time.

None of this was difficult for Rex and me, or for Daffodil, Maria's yellow Lab, who was nearly as receptive to training as Rex. Too bad I couldn't say the same for the others.

Romeo, the chocolate Lab, was turning out to be the poster boy for the "beautiful but dumb" stereotype. He couldn't seem to understand "forward." He kept circling and sniffing at Megan's knee. Which frustrated her to no end. She tugged at him repeatedly, but that only got him to stand still, not move forward.

Trey's corgi, the diminutive Clark Kent, was relentless in his pursuit of Daffodil. No amount of clicking, Pup-Peroni, Snausages, or even Yummy Chummy Bacon Bits could trump his single-mindedness. Trey was worse than Megan as a trainer. He kept scolding the poor pup, "Clark Kent, no! Stop it!" while yanking the leash. LuLu was forced to give them all her attention, to show Trey how to gently correct the dog, not scold him. Dogs learn by praise, not punishment.

They certainly don't learn if you're not teaching them. That was the situation with the fearsome foursome: Lissa and Chainsaw, JJ and Otis. They trailed behind us, at least half a block away. It took a moment to see why. They'd stopped to stare at one of the houses.

Really? They are going to break into this one? In the middle of a class? Besides, the house—a small, one-story beige stucco with a postage-stamp-sized lawn—was not exactly a burglar's dream house. To me the house didn't look like much, but maybe to Lissa it was a palace.

Rex and I did a U-turn and jogged back toward

Lissa and JJ. I was still too far away to hear much when they began to argue. It didn't matter. Their body language spoke volumes—set on high.

Lissa had tossed Chainsaw's leash on the ground and started down the driveway, furiously motioning for JJ to follow.

JJ wasn't into it. He strode after her, trying to grab her arm and, it looked like, pull her away. Lissa was resisting, holding her ground.

By now Rex and I were just a few yards away. Did I yell out to them? Let them know I was watching? If you suspect a crime's about to be committed and don't say anything, isn't that withholding information? Isn't that exactly what JJ was doing with my dad's case?

But were they really planning to break in? I should have either interfered—or walked away.

Instead, I just stood there like an idiot. Any minute, they could turn and see me.

"There's a time to be brave and a time to cave." That wasn't Rex; it was my dad's voice in my head. "If you know something is the right thing to do, even if you're scared, do it anyway. But if doing it puts you in immediate danger, run away, fast. I trust you to know the difference."

I didn't.

"What do you want to do?" This time, it was Rex.

"Not sure. What do you think?" I actually asked this of a dog.

"Your call, Detective Abernathy."

In the end, JJ made the call. He yanked Lissa around, put Chainsaw's leash in her hand, and marched her back toward the group. Too bad. I would've liked to catch him in a crime. I'd have been on the phone to the cops in a blink of an eye.

Rex, reading my mind, said, "He stopped her from breaking into someone's house. Maybe he's not as bad as you want to think."

I countered, "Or maybe he's not stupid enough to do it in broad daylight. Maybe they'll both go back tonight." Even as I said it, however, my instinct told me no—whatever Lissa was going to do, it wasn't going to involve JJ.

When Lissa and JJ rejoined the group, I laser-focused on them. The two were quick studies and had their dogs moving forward in a straight line and stopping at curbs in a lot less time than it took, say, Romeo or Clark Kent.

They apparently had not hugged it out, though. The tension between JJ and Lissa was thick as layered cheesecake. Every time she looked at him, she scowled.

LuLu was now ready to teach us how the dogs lead

a blind person across the street. I stole nervous glances at Lissa and JJ as we walked a few blocks farther until we came to a wide, busy avenue and gathered at the nearest intersection. The light was red.

"Don't look at what color the light is," LuLu instructed. "I want you to listen—and think. A blind person can't see the colors. Neither can a dog. How does a guiding-eyes dog know when it's safe to cross the street?"

The light was now green. The "Walk" sign lit up, but we stayed put. The light changed back to red, then after a while, green again. Suddenly, it hit me and I blurted, "When the light facing us is green, the traffic in front of us stops and it's quiet. When it's red, there's the noise of the traffic flow. It has nothing to do with the colors of the light."

A broad smile brought out crinkles around LuLu's eyes. "That's exactly it! Well done, Grace!"

I looked at Rex. He was beaming, his eyes actually twinkled, and his tail waved like a palm tree in a wild windstorm.

"But what if they come to an intersection and it's quiet?" asked Megan. "How do they know how much longer they have until the light's going to change?"

"Good question," LuLu said.

"They just wait," Maria guessed. "They wait until they hear the traffic surge, and as soon as the sound stops, and they've checked that no cars are coming, they know they've got enough time to cross."

"They wait through an entire traffic cycle before crossing. It takes a little longer, but it's the safest way," LuLu recited. "When in doubt, wait it out."

·· 10 ··

Truth or Dare

As a reward for an excellent session, LuLu let us out early. Six trainers and six dogs tromped out of the building together. After fifteen minutes, two were left standing and waiting. Neither JJ nor I had been able to reach our rides for an earlier pickup. Neither of us was happy about it. But I wasn't about to let an opportunity slip by. I *would* confront him.

Only now that I had him, all the things I thought I'd say went flying out of my head. So I went with the first thing that came to mind.

"That whole thing today with Lissa, I couldn't help overhearing." Big lie.

"Overhearing what?" He looked annoyed.

I backpedaled. After all, I hadn't overheard anything: Rex had. I wasn't on firm ground here, but I went for it. "I got the distinct impression she was about to break into someone's house."

JJ, taller than me by a head, stared at something well over mine. I couldn't even tell if he was listening, so I said, a little louder, "Was she?"

This time, he shrugged and mumbled dismissively, "No idea, man."

Okay, now I was annoyed. "Right, you have a history of not knowing what's going on right in front of you."

That got his attention, and his defenses up. "What's that supposed to mean?"

"I think you know."

"Don't know what you're talking about." *Really? Like when my dad got shot—you were right there, but somehow convinced the cops that you didn't see what really happened.*

I would've gotten in his face if I were taller. I took a half step closer and with all the bravado I could muster, I said, "Again, I think you do."

Too late, it hit me that I didn't know what JJ was really capable of. What if his annoyance turned to anger? Sure, we had big dogs at our feet—big dogs who were now plopped out, fast asleep on the sidewalk.

I sucked in a breath. If he took one step toward me—I'd turn around and run as fast as I could.

JJ didn't move. Instead, he gazed into the distance and said, "Look, I wasn't even in the car that day, if that's what you mean. I don't know how your old man went down."

I was stunned into silence. How could he say he wasn't in the car—that was the one thing he'd admitted to. Now he was taking it back? Unacceptable!

"You're lying!" I accused him, forgetting to be scared. "Why'd you tell the cops you were there if you weren't? Why put yourself at the scene of the crime?"

JJ's nerves were starting to show. He shifted his weight from one foot to the other and rubbed the back of his neck with his arm.

"Why confess to being there if you weren't?" I repeated.

His eyes skated back and forth. I bet he was hoping his ride would pull up right then. It didn't. There was no escape at hand.

"Look, my brother was there, okay? It was him in the backseat, not me. But he's got kind of a record, and I didn't want the cops looking at him. Besides, he didn't *do* anything. The way it worked out, I didn't get in trouble and neither did he. So it's win-win."

My jaw fell to the ground, my eyes began to sting. Win-win?

JJ noticed—and sort of apologized. "That came out wrong."

At least that's what I think he said. I couldn't hear

over the screeching of a car's brakes coming just a second too late—its front tires were already up on the pavement—and someone shouting at JJ, "Yo—wu-ss-ee! Get your ass in gear!"

I nearly vomited. So this was JJ's ride—two gang members, both all too memorable from the days of sitting behind the one-way glass watching them being interrogated.

"Oh, man—look who's with him—the cop's kid!" blared the guy in the passenger seat. Chris. I was surprised—I remembered them, but I didn't think they'd know me.

"What're you doing with her?" demanded the driver, the pock-faced Hector Lowe. Or lowlife, as I thought of him.

"Not cool, man," said Chris.

"Get that girly dog and get in the car," barked Hector.

Without a word, or a second glance, JJ obeyed. So much for my brilliant plan to get JJ to fess up. I was left standing on the sidewalk with a head full of questions and fewer answers than I'd ever had.

Oh, and a talking dog. Can't forget that.

∾

"Earth to Grace Abernathy!" Regan had pulled up to the curb.

"What?" I said, opening the back door for Rex, taking shotgun for myself.

"I've been talking to you."

"You just got here," I stammered, trying to shove JJ's big reveal to the back of my mind—for now. I searched for something mundane to say, and found it on the seat: Regan's cell phone, open to a chat. "Tell me you weren't driving and texting."

"Stay on topic," she admonished me.

"Which is . . . ?"

"Mom's necklace." Regan's voice was tinged with annoyance. "It was hanging off the screen of my laptop. Mom didn't know anything about it. Did you put it there?"

On Friday—three days ago. I'd about given up that Regan was even going to mention it.

"I did, because—" I was just about to explain when Regan accused me, "The laptop was open. Were you eavesdropping, too?"

Eavesdropping? It was official. My sister had fertilizer for brains. "Eavesdropping means secretly listening in on someone. And no, I wasn't snooping." I only half lied. She didn't need to know I read her essay.

"Were you trying to bedazzle my screen, then?" she guessed, changing lanes while eyeing me.

I told her to keep her eyes on the road. Then,

choosing my words carefully, I said, "I got the necklace from Sheena."

Again Regan turned to look at me quizzically.

"Please watch the road," I said. "And let me explain."

Only . . . I didn't *have* a believable explanation for why I'd gone to Mom's room and caught Sheena red-handed. I went with, "I was in my room, and I heard noise coming from Mom's room."

An excuse that wouldn't hold up under questioning—the music was too loud for me to have heard anything—but Regan was no Sherlock Holmes.

"I went to investigate. I took Rex."

"Your point?"

"I found Sheena pawing through Mom's jewelry. She was checking out that necklace. She was going to steal it."

"You're delusional."

"That's what *I* thought," I agreed, remembering. "Then I asked her what she was doing, and she goes, 'I was on my way to the bathroom.' Right—like the most direct route is through Mom's jewelry box."

"You're not making any sense, Grace."

That's because none of this makes any sense! I wanted to scream. But I held it together and plowed on.

"Rex . . . well, he must have sensed something. He sort of growled at her, and she, uh, dropped her purse. I couldn't believe my eyes—a bunch of Mom's stuff fell out, including"—I hesitated, getting indignant now— "Dad's wedding ring."

Regan jerked the wheel, and we cut into the right lane, missing a UPS truck by inches. She mashed her lips together and defaulted to a second-grade put-down: "You're a big fat liar."

I don't lie. If you knew at least one thing about me, you'd know that. A tiny bubble of self-pity threatened to burst, but I choked it down. "Why would I make this up?" I croaked.

"I don't know!" She sounded exasperated. One hand flew off the steering wheel. "You want to punish me for having a few friends over. You're jealous . . . or something. Besides, you never liked Sheena."

Tiny beads of sweat tarnished Regan's smooth, unfettered forehead. Translation: she was starting to have doubts. For now, that would have to do.

Then my sister threw me for a loop of her own. A biggie.

"So what are you going to do about your grades?"

My stomach plunged. She knew. "Did the school call Mom?" I asked in a small voice.

"They left a message. I erased it."

I did a double take. "Why?"

"I don't want to upset her. Not without giving you a chance to pull yourself out of this mess you've created."

"What if I don't want to?" I said belligerently.

She gave me a sideways glance. "Of course you want to. Besides, if Mom finds out, she'll ground you and your training days will be over."

"Always an 'advantage-Regan' agenda," I grumbled.

"It's not about me," she lied. "Training that dog is good for you."

"And frees *you* up to do whatever it is you actually do," I retorted.

"It was Dad's idea, you know, training a service dog," she said slowly as she made a left turn on Center Street.

"No, it wasn't," I contradicted. "I never heard him say anything about it." True, Mom had said he sometimes enrolled at-risk kids into the program, but he'd never mentioned it to me.

"He talked to me, too, you know," Regan said quietly.

"Of course he talked to you. You're his daughter."

Was his daughter. Neither of us said it. But I couldn't drop it. No way did Regan and Dad share stuff I didn't know about. I huffed, "So you're saying Dad told you to train a service dog so your college application would look good?"

She squirmed. "Not exactly, maybe. But I think he would totally approve."

"I don't think so, Regan, not for that reason. It's self-serving."

"I'm not as smart as you are, Grace," she said

heatedly. "I sweat for every decent grade I get. I tank on standardized tests in spite of all the tutors Mom and Dad hired for me. To get into Parsons, I need this kind of advantage. Dad understood, he really did. He wanted me to follow my dream."

Lost

Let's walk home!" Rex exclaimed the following Friday after class. "Waiting for Regan is boring."

"It's too far," I said, stifling a yawn.

"I know a shortcut!" Rex's dust-mop tail wagged eagerly.

"You do? Do you have a built-in GPS chip you haven't told me about?" Anyway, no.

It had been a tire-melting day with temperatures matching the kind of test scores I used to get—high nineties. I raked my fingers through my limp hair and yawned again. Today's lesson had been particularly tedious. We'd spent most of it waiting for the other dogs to learn how to target, or zero in on a specific item, retrieve it, and return it. LuLu explained that this exercise is so our dogs will be able to go shopping with their new partners, pick items off the shelf, and place them in a shopping basket. It's a very cool skill but learned only with a lot of practice. The commands "watch me," "get it," "hold," "give it," and "good boy!" played like a loop in my head.

"Let's go," Rex insisted, tugging on the leash.

"Regan will be here any minute."

"She can pick us up en route," Rex replied.

"En route? You speak French, too?" I said, almost smiling.

"I'm not your average Scooby-Doo," Rex said puckishly.

"You're more like Scooby-Don't."

"Oh, come on, Tracey, be adventurous! Get out of your rut! Exercise is good for the soul!"

I groaned. "You're gonna keep talking until I give in, aren't you?"

The dog looked like the Cheshire cat.

We crossed the wide boulevard and made our way west past the Publix supermarket, the CVS pharmacy, and Cold Stone Creamery. We wove through Gregory's Landing, a posh complex surrounding a manicured golf course. We crossed route A1A, and cut through a neighborhood called Jupiter Pines, where every house matched the one next to it.

I gazed up at the sky. An amber sun was setting. It

reminded me of a picture my dad once took. We'd gone to the beach, and Dad had caught a candid of Mom gazing out into the ocean; the sun was just this exact color.

Mom loves seeing the sunrise over the ocean; she says it's the most awe-inspiring, beautiful sight in the world. My dad promised that if we ever won the lottery (which was doubtful since we didn't play), he'd buy her a house on Jupiter Island, the ritziest part of our town, where every home is beachfront and you could watch the sun rise every single day if you got up early enough.

Dad liked being by the water, too, but for him, night-fall was way cooler. He loved watching the moonbeams streaking the ink-black ocean. "There's just something mystical about that, Gracie," he once mused. It was a strange comment from him, since my dad was the ulti-mate "prove it and I'll believe it" realist. He didn't go for any of that "new-agey, mystical, woo-woo" stuff. Me neither.

"So you're reading that book about the pig," Rex said, trotting beside me.

"Pig?" I repeated, momentarily confused. "You mean *The Pigman & Me.*"

"And?" the dog prompted.

And what? Did I like it? Not really. I was reading it, as Rex no doubt knew, because Mr. Kassan said he'd pass me if I did a report on it, and didn't flake on future assignments. I chose the shortest book on the list.

I felt sick every time I thought about school. If my dad knew I was flunking . . . well, he wouldn't believe it. "Not my Gracie," I could hear him saying. "She's way too smart. You must have her confused with someone else."

"I miss him." My words sounded hollow and hoarse.

Rex stopped dead in his tracks, almost like a cartoon dog. He whirled around and clomped his weighty front paws down on my flip-flopped feet. Staring at me with big, marbled brown eyes, he said, "I can listen."

"Not like him." I slipped my feet out from under his paws and continued walking. I don't know how long after that—five minutes? Fifteen?—when I realized we were no longer anywhere I recognized. We'd taken a turnoff somewhere, perhaps back on Indiantown Road, or maybe Haverhill, and ended up in an unfamiliar neighborhood.

There were no sidewalks. Jaggedy lawns wild with weeds spread all the way up to the street. The houses were set far apart; not one had a paved driveway. Many had foreclosure signs, and worse, one after the other was run-down or boarded up and abandoned altogether. I checked the time. Over an hour had gone by since we'd left Canine Connections. Why weren't we home? And why hadn't I heard from my sister?

"Don't worry," Rex assured me. "I know exactly where we are."

"Share it," I demanded. Just then, some unidentifiable small woodland creature skittered right in front of me and I jumped ten feet off the ground. *I don't think we're in Kansas anymore, Toto* went through my head. But neither my head nor I found it funny.

"Relax, Francie, we're cutting through Prosperity Farms. You know it."

Clarification: I know *of* it: A. People say it used to be a nice, woodsy, rural area. B. Despite its hopeful name, neither the area nor anyone in it ever prospered. Now, it's run-down, depleted, and mostly deserted. C. My mom would be freaked out if she knew I was here, and only partly because D. it's nowhere near where I live.

E. If you believe the TV news, gangs run rampant and dead bodies turn up here with alarming frequency.

"Rex," I growled through gritted teeth, "this is not the way home. What are we doing here?"

"It's garbage pickup day—they'll have good snacks!" he said jauntily, nosing a nearby garbage can. "Once I found a whole turkey carcass. Of course, that was right after Thanksgiving and . . ."

"No way! I can't believe I let you drag me here." My stomach twisted into a knot of panic. Why hadn't Regan called? Or maybe she had, and I hadn't heard the phone? She'd kill me.

With mounting fear, I slipped my cell phone out of my pocket and got the answer I dreaded: no bars. No service. I needed to orient myself. As we approached a corner, I looked up at the street sign: 159th Road. I checked the cross street: 159th Lane. I was officially creeped out.

I dragged Rex to the next intersection, and was hit with the same feeling I had when I first heard him talking to me: I've lost my mind. It read: 159th Court. If I hadn't gone crazy, then I'd entered the Twilight Zone, only not the one with sexy vampires and ripped werewolves. The one from that classic TV series where people end up on staircases with no exits, in elevators that never stop at your floor, in towns that don't exist.

Rex, meanwhile, had hit paydirt: a juicy steak bone that must've spilled over from someone's unlidded garbage can.

"Rex!" I stomped my foot. "Put that down and take me back the way we came. Now!"

"No problem," he said, gnawing the bone. "Just follow me."

"That's what got me into trouble in the first place," I grumbled, knowing my options were severely limited. We'd trained the dogs to lead blind people; now, blindly, I followed the dog.

Obsessively I checked for the return of bars on my phone.

"Come this way." Rex directed me to turn onto 149th

Street. "I'm almost sure this cut through will take us to your house. Toward it, anyway," he amended.

He's almost *sure? It's almost nightfall! I'm about ready to return him to the shelter!* We zigged and we zagged, until I felt like I was trapped in a maze with no exit. I needed to find a main thoroughfare. Failing that, I needed a landline.

"Hey, there's a light on in this house." Rex pointed his snout toward a shabbily shingled house with a sagging front porch. "Why not see if they'll let you use the phone? Regan might be getting nervous by now."

I wanted to strangle the dog. Might be? I eyed the house warily. The windows were bare, and yes, there was clearly a light on inside. Cars were parked at random angles in the driveway and on the front lawn. As we approached, I could hear the insistent thump of some kind of techno-metal music.

People were home—but did I really want to find out who?

"I don't see any other houses with lights on," Rex prompted as I hesitated. "Unless you want to walk farther, to, say, 149th Way?"

What would Dad say to do in this situation? I pictured my big burly dad narrowing his eyes so his caterpillar eyebrows knitted together. This totally qualified as a scary situation. Should I be brave and ring the doorbell? Or run? I scoured my brain for some other Dad-sanctioned advice. All I came up with was, "Gracie, if you feel fear, there's probably a good reason. Act on it."

But . . . act how? Keep going, or trust that just because the neighborhood is gang territory doesn't mean the big bad wolf lurks behind every door?

I took a deep breath and followed Rex up two dilapidated porch steps and tried to convince myself that maybe a nice, unthreatening person would open the door. Or, failing that, hoped Rex looked ferocious enough to scare off any stranger-danger. For his part, the dog acted unconcerned. Showing off a newly learned skill—not that anyone asked him to—Rex hoisted himself on his hind legs, and using his nose, targeted the doorbell, and pressed. LuLu would have been so proud.

It didn't have the desired effect. All we heard was the insistent *thump-thump* of a backbeat—no ringing of a doorbell. Rex tried again. Still nothing.

Was no one home, contrary to appearances? A part of me was relieved at the prospect. Or was the doorbell broken?

"Go on," Rex directed. "Knock."

As soon as my knuckles hit the door, we heard a series of deep, throaty barks, like those of a large beast. Again, I hoped my canine companion could out-frighten whatever we were about to be greeted with.

Rex had no interest in terrorizing anyone, man or beast. Even as the door opened a crack, Rex rocketed inside the house, whooping for joy. "Otis! I thought it was you. I got a bone! Let's play tug-of-war!"

Only I heard him, of course. And I wasn't reacting, at least not to Rex. The boy who'd answered my knock had eyes as black as olives, sharp cheekbones, and a head full of thick, black hair.

Anger and fear collided and squished my heart.

Not him. Not on his turf. Not in the dark. One by one, tentacles of terror coiled around me and squeezed hard. In my head, I whipped around and ran. But in reality, I stood there, quaking. And then, just for a split second, JJ Pico's coal-colored eyes reflected something I never imagined in a boy like him: fear.

"What're you doing here?" He sounded more scared than scary.

"I made a mistake," I said, trying to compose myself. "Rex! Let's go."

Rex was nowhere to be seen. He and Otis had rough-housed their way deeper inside the house. No way was I going after them. I cupped my hands around my mouth and called, "Rex! Come! Now!"

If Rex heard, he ignored me.

"Really, man, what are you doing here?" JJ demanded, nervously peering over his shoulder. He wasn't looking for the dogs. The cars on the lawn, the music—JJ had company.

"Look," I said, trying to hold it together, "we got lost on the way home and . . ." I trailed off.

"No kidding, Magellan. You've got to be miles from wherever you live."

"I need a landline," I admitted. "It was just random that I rang your doorbell. Anyway, we're going. Rex!"

Understanding crossed his face just then. He tilted his head up just slightly and lowered his voice. "Wait here. I'll get you the phone—but don't even think of calling the cops or anything. Because I was cleared . . ." It was his turn to trail off.

A burning fury crept up my neck. JJ Pico had been released without any criminal charges against him. But even if he'd lied about being in the car that day, his brother *had* been. And brothers brag—JJ had to know something. I bet he thinks I know more, too. Why else would he seem so nervous about my surprise appearance?

"Swear you won't call the cops, I'll give you the phone," he repeated.

"I don't want anything from you," I snarled. "Just my dog."

"Don't be stupid," JJ said. "You're lost in this crap neighborhood. Stay there." He turned and strode inside.

It would have been the moment to flee—even without

Rex. But the idea of returning to the nightmare maze of streets was enough to keep me rooted.

A minute later, JJ returned bearing a cordless phone. "Make it quick."

My fingers were shaking as I punched in Regan's number. Luckily, she picked it up on the first ring, and I managed to tell her where I was. I disconnected over her outraged reprimands. "Thank you," I mumbled, handing the phone back to JJ.

"Yo, man, who's the guest?" a voice from down the darkened hallway called out.

"JJ got company? Bring her inside," another voice chimed in.

Way before my head got the message, my heart started to pound. Without seeing them, I knew who was there. Panic rose up in me and I took a step back.

Not far enough. A face to match the menacing voice materialized over JJ's shoulder. I didn't recognize this guy, who wore his greasy hair in a ponytail, but I did make a gutsy guess. "Is this your brother?"

JJ's jaw dropped, but before he could say anything, a torrent of laughter poured from ponytail guy. "She thinks I'm Tommy? That's a hoot, man."

I started to form a question, but was interrupted by the appearance of the heinous Hector, clutching a beer and bearing an explanation. "JJ's brother is in jail.

Surprised, with all your connections," he sneered, "you don't know that. Been there for two years."

"Hey." Chris joined the crowd at the front door. "Her again? What's going on, man? Why you hangin' with the cop's kid?"

"Not anymore." Hector snickered. "Cop's dead."

Something inside me snapped. With a stupidity I didn't know I had, I reared back and spit in Hector's face. I got him in the eye.

Hector shoved JJ out of the way and came at me. I was a dead girl . . .

. . . Or would have been, but three things got between Hector and me: a white poodle, a raggedy mutt—and JJ Pico.

The dogs were barking wildly, JJ was shouting, and I was ready to hurl another loogey when the screech of Regan's tires as she came flying around the corner on two wheels sent me and Rex bolting down the driveway.

·· 12 ··

What if I'm Not Crazy?

There was no question of dinner that night. I was choked with anger. I was furious at JJ for his bold-faced lie—he *had* been in the car with those monsters, and he *knew* who had pulled the gun. I was enraged at the police for not convicting them in the first place, and at Regan for always being late. Mostly I was infuriated with myself for moronically following the dog. I stormed off to my room, where I could lock myself in, and everyone else out. Too wound up to sit still, I paced, kicking hard at the piles of stuff littering the floor, the inside-out clothes, smelly socks, unlaced sneakers, Mom's scrapbooks, the book I was trying to read for school, and random photos. What was once merely messy was now an official trash heap: the detritus of my life for the past six months.

It isn't fair! I wanted to punch the walls, throw the window open, and scream so loudly that when I stopped everything would be back to the way it used to be.

I'm not a tantrum thrower. I never was. We already had one drama queen in the family. I guess I figured there wasn't room for two. When I was really young, and succumbed to the occasional meltdown, I could count on a predictable pattern. I'd get a time-out, or denied TV, or be grounded, but I knew my dad would eventually show up bearing a bowl of ice cream. It was always vanilla fudge, my favorite. That was his signal: I'd served my time, all was forgiven, and life could go back to normal.

When I got older and faced some injustice, I called Mercy, or Jazz, or even Kendra and went on a venting spree until I was calm. Failing that, at least I could usually lose myself in a book, a movie, a school assignment if necessary. I used to be able to drown out the world by turning the music way up. I had coping skills.

Skills that had deserted me now. I couldn't even cry.

"Let me in, please, Niecy, I can explain everything." On the other side of the door, Rex whimpered. As far as I was concerned, he could whine all night. My room was off-limits to him.

Eventually, I stopped pacing and kicking, slid down the wall, and curled into a ball. A picture of me and my dad, taken at the sixth-grade father-daughter dance, was sticking out of a pile on the floor. I picked it up. Between the wrong poufy dress and worst haircut ever and pre-contact lenses, I looked like a frizz-topped matzo ball with bad glasses. My expression was one of appropriate mortification.

My dad might have had his arm around an Olympic gold medalist or a rock star: He was beaming with pride. His cheek-to-cheek smile lit up the room. His eyes, large and round and sky blue, sparkled.

Regan's eyes. Ironic how she'd inherited my dad's exact coloring but not an iota of his other traits. At the memorials, they called my dad "tough but fair." At home he was the softy. My mom had been the disciplinarian.

"How could you leave me?" I demanded of the picture. The only response was Rex, scratching at the door.

"Go away!" I growled, and went to work on the photo, ripping it again and again, into a million little pieces.

"I have to talk to you!" Rex pleaded.

Dogs don't talk.

"I can explain . . ."

Dogs don't lead unsuspecting thirteen-year-olds to bad neighborhoods.

". . . about JJ."

And they don't lead victims to predators.

Believing Rex did all those things proved I'd sailed past merely wacko into crazy town.

And I was flunking out of school.

If nothing else was real, that was. The copy of *The Pigman & Me* stuck out from under a balled-up T-shirt, mocking me.

What if I'm not crazy?

Ping! A sliver of a thought popped up in a corner of my brain. Like those jarring ads for an upcoming TV show that appear on the bottom of the screen when you're watching something else—small but impossible to ignore.

What if I played it out, just for a minute. That, what? The dog is talking, but only to me. Because, why? He's not really a dog, but some otherworldly being, a spirit, an angel in the body of a mangy mutt. And he's come to me . . . why? I shook my head wildly, fisted my hands, and rubbed hard at my eyes.

I'd gone way too far. There's no such thing as otherworldly beings; neither angels nor devils and especially not dogs-who-are-really-spirits.

"Grace, it's Mom—please let me in."

How long had *she* been at the door? Reluctantly, I uncoiled myself and stood up. I was a mess. Dried sweat had wrinkled my top, my shorts. I swiped tendrils of springy frizz behind my ears.

In contrast, Mom was put together, all made-up, freshly shampooed hair, cute outfit. She'd even gotten a manicure, I noticed. She was holding a tray with my dinner.

I'm not hungry, I wanted to say, but the words never came out. The aroma was tantalizing. She'd made chicken, steamed mixed vegetables, and—this is what made my mouth water against my will—shoestring french fries. That was Dad's from-scratch specialty. He used to peel potatoes, put them through a special slicer called a mandolin to get them really thin, and then deep-fry them. My mom claimed to be fried-food averse, but even she could never resist Dad's crunchy-salty potatoes. That she attempted to make them herself sent my battered heart plunging.

"I'll put this down on your desk," she said, crossing the room. She managed to avoid stepping on anything, and tactfully, didn't comment on the waste heap.

"Thanks," I said, swiping a couple of T-shirts off the floor and tossing them on my bed. Out of the corner of my eye I saw Rex slink in.

"I know you're mad at your sister," Mom said, "and it sounds like you have good reason, but you can't let anger consume you."

"What did Regan tell you?" I asked, picking at a fry.

"That she was so late picking you up, you walked home."

"That's all?" I asked warily.

"There's no excuse for her constant tardiness," Mom declared with a toss of her curls.

"This time it wasn't all Regan's fault."

But Mom was just warming up. "I've let your sister slip by with too few responsibilities. That's got to change, especially since"—she blinked—"it's just the three of us now."

A large lump formed in my throat, thwarting a second fry from sliding down.

"I'm done with asking, or suggesting. I'm *insisting* Regan take over Rex's training. Which she should have been doing from the start. Anyway, she can't be late picking herself up." Mom's attempt at a lighthearted moment landed with a thud.

I sank into the chair by my desk and tried to unboggle my mind. Regan, who'd given me a full verbal thrashing on the ride home, didn't bust me about ending up in Prosperity Farms—at JJ Pico's house, no less. She took the heat herself. Who was she protecting, Mom or me?

Rex, who'd never taken his eyes off my dinner, offered, "You can't let Regan take me to class. Tell her it's helping you."

Mom glanced down at Rex. "What are you barking at?"

Which Rex took to mean: yes, you *can* have chicken. He rested his snout dangerously near the tray.

"Oh, no, you don't," Mom admonished. "This is Grace's dinner. You had yours."

"It's fine, Mom. Really. I mean . . . taking him to training class. I think it might be"—I hesitated—"you know, helping me a little." I stuffed four fries into my mouth this time. They needed salt.

She looked perplexed, but went into auto-mom mode. "Eat some chicken, too."

"It was a stupid idea to walk home," I conceded. "It wasn't Regan's fault that I didn't wait for her."

"I don't want to stop you from working with the dog, but . . ." She paused. "Your sister has to go, too. Regan has to be there for you."

She kind of *is*. That's the strangest part of all. As I ate—the chicken wasn't half bad, though the vegetables hadn't quite been cooked through—I wondered what Regan was up to. She hadn't busted me for flunking out, and now she didn't say where she'd picked me up. Did she think we'd made some silent pact? If I didn't mention Sheena's thievery, she'd cover for me?

When my mom left, I laced into Rex. "Who invited you in here?"

"The door was open," he said innocently.

"Not for you it wasn't. I'm mad at you!"

"Me? Why?"

"You led me right to JJ's door."

"It wasn't on purpose," Rex said defensively, eyeing the chicken.

"It's the mother of all coincidences, then, isn't it?"

"I told you, it was garbage pickup day."

"Right, we ended up in the most dangerous part of town for a turkey bone."

"Actually, turkey's not that good for dogs; there's that whole tryptophan thing. Do you know about that?"

I glowered at the dog. He looked hurt. "Don't give me that sad-eyed puppy face," I warned him.

"I don't see why you're so mad at me. How could I even know where that boy lived?"

Isn't *that* the question.

"But as long as we did end up there," Rex resumed, "I have a few thoughts."

"Keep them to yourself."

"JJ's not a bad kid."

"You betrayed me, Rex. I don't know how, or why. But Dad said I should always trust my instincts—and something tells me you knew exactly where we were going."

"I have an instinct, too," he piped up.

"No, you just have a stink."

As usual, Rex ignored me and kept right on babbling. "Give the kid a chance. He's okay, really. I feel it in my bones. Oh, and speaking of bones, if you're not eating that one . . ."

I moved the half-gnawed thigh out of his reach.

"He doesn't have a father either. He worshipped yours."

JJ didn't even know my dad, I wanted to shoot back at

Rex. But the truth is, I didn't know if that was true. I only wanted it to be.

"Why don't you just ask him who had the gun?" Rex said as casually as if he were suggesting I ask Kendra how she gets the shine in her hair.

"Ask him?" I repeated. "What good will that do me? He just proved he's a—" I almost echoed Regan, "big fat liar," but stopped myself. I came out with the way better "slimeball."

"Oh, come on, Lacey, you're gonna get derailed over *one* lie? You think your dad would have just let it go at that?"

Rex the talking dog is comparing me, a torn-apart thirteen-year-old, to my dad? I had nothing of my dad's skills.

"Make him tell you the truth."

You owe it to him. That wasn't Rex's voice in my head. It was my own.

Meanwhile, Rex had worked his way through half the chicken.

·· 13 ··

Mall Tease

The Gardens is our neighborhood mall. It's a two-story superdome of luxury anchored by the upscale department stores Nordstrom, Saks, and Bloomingdale's. Boutiques of such chic designers as Louis Vuitton, Gucci, Burberry, and Chanel dot the main corridor. Sure, there's a token JCPenney, three varieties of the Gap, and a food court, but for the most part the fashion is outrageous, the prices obscene. It's not a place you'd ever find me. Unless I couldn't avoid it.

Sunday morning, I had no choice but to be there. Taking our dogs to the mall to get them used to crowds, noise, and kiddie chaos was a Canine Connections assignment. By Mom's decree, Regan had to come, but ordering my fashion-obsessed sib to a fancy mall didn't seem like the best way to force her into taking responsibility.

The automatic doors parted, Regan departed to power shop.

Rex and I met up with the rest of our class by the elevator. Correction: the rest of our class minus JJ and Otis. In spite of Rex's insistence that I corner JJ and demand to know what really happened, his absence worked for me. Already I was more comfortable.

Because our dogs might be paired with a person confined to a wheelchair and unable to use an escalator, our first task was to teach the dogs to push the elevator call button. We'd practiced in class using a simulator, but this would be the first time using an operational elevator.

Even before we started, we attracted attention. A clutch of shoppers, charmed by the pups-with-a-purpose, had gathered round to watch. Some even obeyed the DON'T PET instruction stitched onto their vests. To the others we explained that petting a service dog is distracting and counterproductive to his training. In a real situation with a disabled person, diverting the dog from its job could prove dangerous.

The warning deterred few people, who couldn't keep their own paws off Romeo, Daffodil, Chainsaw, and even dwarfy Clark Kent. Only Rex went without shopper-strokes: the not-cute factor was in full effect. I found myself actually hurt on his behalf! I knelt and whispered to him, "Don't be upset. These people aren't worth it."

Rex licked my face.

My dog may not inspire *oooh*s and *aaah*s, but as a service dog, he was a superstar. When I gave the command for "side," Rex obediently positioned himself to my right so the elevator button was straight in front of him. Then I showed him the UP button and said, "Reach." Just like we practiced, and he did the other night at JJ's house, Rex hoisted himself up on his hind legs and nosed down hard on the button.

"Good boy!" I praised him, maybe a little too loudly.

When the elevator arrived I told him, "Let's go," and he dutifully led me inside, where he followed the commands to push the 2 button.

"You're the champ!" I overpraised him. When no one was looking, I slipped him a Snausage.

Rex even "tutored" Chainsaw—at least that's how I interpreted the growly sounds of their canine communication. Daffodil and Romeo mastered the assignment with few corrections and earned lavish praise. Only Clark Kent, whose stunted legs prevented him from getting up high enough to press the button, couldn't complete the task.

Next up was retrieval. We were to drop a water bottle on the floor while saying, "Look." Then, "Get it" and "Bring it to me."

Eventually, the dogs will be able to accompany their new partners on real shopping trips and pull specific items off the shelves or racks—very, very cool. I was looking forward to next week, when our field trip was to a grocery store to test out this "look," "get it," and "bring it to me" skill in a real store. But for now, our purpose was to practice focusing amid distractions, and be sure they didn't get startled at loud noises or interruptions.

As late morning drifted into early afternoon, the mall got more crowded. Distractions abounded. Toddlers in strollers begged to pet the dogs or offer them snacks, a serious doggy-temptation. A pack of young girls dangerously swinging shopping bags came too close to Romeo and brushed his tail, which caused the chocolate Lab to whirl around, startled. Countless customers on cell phones breezed by, oblivious to the fact that they were getting between the dogs and their water bottles.

Each time one of our dogs got distracted, we were to gently bring them back to the job at hand. When they followed the command correctly, they got a reward—praise, hugs, petting. And in Rex's case (okay, I felt a little sorry for him), a treat.

Of course my chowhound was most excited about today's final destination—the food court. The lesson, a little complicated, involved ordering lunch. We'd teach the dogs to pay and deliver the food to us. Beforehand, we put a credit card in our pockets or purses where the dog could get at it. As soon as we placed our orders, the dogs were to get up on their hind legs and give the credit card to the cashier. The food would be placed in a to-go bag so the dog could bring it to us.

The Gardens' food court was horseshoe shaped with stalls around the perimeter and seating in the middle. Aside from the obligatory Starbucks (this mall had one on each floor), selections included pizza, gyros, subs, teriyaki, cookies, ice cream, and salad.

"Let's talk turkey!" Rex exclaimed as we came to the very first stand—a sandwich and salad shop actually called Let's Talk Turkey. I was headed for the counter when Rex suddenly yanked me away. "No, wait, I haven't had pizza in forever. Oh, I'd give my soul for a slice!"

Obligingly, I pivoted and headed for Sbarro, but again Rex hesitated, overwhelmed by the profusion of savory smells. I allowed the litany of "I want ice cream! No, cookies! Wait, I must experience the Teriyaki Experience!" go on for a few minutes, attracting confused stares of passersby as the dog yanked me in different directions. Finally, I made an executive decision: I'd order a turkey Caesar wrap and share the croutons with Rex. It was neat and small—something he could carry in a to-go bag, and I could eat quickly with a minimum of mess. If I texted Regan now, we could be out the door in ten minutes.

We might have, too, only we got ambushed.

"Grace! Hi—over here!" Mercy was half sitting, half standing, waving excitedly. The Gardens is not Mercy's usual haunt. She's more of a vintage store girl, so I wasn't surprised to see she had company. Jasmine and Kendra had spotted me, too. My hoped-for ten minutes had just inflated into a half hour. Reluctantly, I walked over to them, forging a smile.

"So this is the dog you're training!" Jasmine squealed, trying to not look appalled as she regarded his scraggly muzzle and chaotically colored coat. "He's so . . . uh . . . alert!"

Rex posed proudly.

"Does he bite?" Kendra wanted to know, backing slowly into her seat.

Only if you're holding a pork chop, I wanted to say. Neither girl petted him.

"This is Rex." I explained our reason for being at the Gardens.

Mercy knelt and scritched the underside of the dog's chin. "Hey there, Rex," she cooed. "It's nice to meet you finally!" Rex responded by stretching out his neck and making a doggy-bliss sound.

"You are so sitting with us," Mercy pronounced. "Unless you have to eat with the others?" She gestured to our classmates, gathered around a too-small table with their dogs obediently lying beneath their seats.

"Yes! Let's sit here!" Rex ruffed. "It's about time I met your friends."

You just want to beg off their trays, I almost said out loud. Rex knew full well that service dogs in training should never be fed table scraps. He calculated—correctly—my friends did not know this rule.

Within minutes, he'd hoovered pizza from Jazz, burger bits from Mercy, and most of a teriyaki kebab from Kendra, who'd apparently lost her appetite.

"We were studying for the social studies test," Mercy explained, biting messily into her burger. "Then Kendra talked us into a shopping break."

"There's this one layered mini and sparkled tank outfit I *have* to have." Kendra made it sound as if she had no choice. "I'm actually deciding between that and a really cute ruffled dress I got at BCBG. It's the same blue as my polish." She held up her hand—her nails were painted Smurf blue. "Either one would look amazing at the dance."

"You're going, right?" Jasmine looked at me hopefully.

Wrong.

"Oh, come on, Grace," urged Jasmine. "You only get one chance to go to an eighth-grade dance."

Not necessarily. At the rate I was going, I might be doing eighth grade all over again. I bit into the turkey wrap, but it was dry and I had trouble getting it down.

Kendra chatted on obliviously. "I'm going to try them on at Jasmine's house. Come and help me choose?"

She stole a glance at Rex. "You can drop him at home first if you want."

"You should come!" Mercy exclaimed. "We're all going to model our outfits and then get back to quizzing each other. We could use you."

I hadn't shared the sorry state of my grades with anyone. But it wasn't hard to figure out, provided you were paying attention to me. Mercy clearly was. I don't know why I did it—right in the middle of the food court at the mall—but something made me blurt, "I don't think studying for one test is going to help."

Jasmine eyed me quizzically.

"How bad is it?" asked Mercy carefully.

"Flunking out bad." There, I said it. They say confession is good for the soul, but I have to confess, neither me nor my soul felt one bit better.

"What does that mean?" asked Kendra, never the brightest light on the Christmas tree.

"Summer school?" guessed Jasmine.

I felt my throat closing, but I managed to croak out, "Repeating the year."

"No. Way." Mercy said it with scary conviction. "Not. Gonna. Happen."

"So says the Magic 8 Ball?" That came out more sarcastically than I intended.

Mercy ignored my snark and gave Jasmine and Kendra a look. We knew what it meant: you're all going to do exactly what I say. Mercy turned to me. "You're not gonna fail because we're not gonna let you. The way I see it, your grades were amazing until your dad died. That means we need to get you up to speed for only this past semester. That's nothing. I tutor kids who are way further behind."

If I could have found it inside me, I would have hugged Mercy. Not only for making it sound like the impossible was possible, but for just coming out and saying "your dad died." A statement of fact. When everyone else around me still acted as if vagueing it up or ignoring it would make it less true.

"I'll take social studies and science. I'm getting As in those." Mercy nudged Jasmine. "You're acing French, right? Can you work with Grace so she passes the final?"

"*Mais bien sur,*" Jazz agreed, kicking into scrambled Franglish. "*Après Grace aidez Kendra* and *moi* choose *les chemises kill-aire!*"

"I'm reading a book for language arts," I mentioned. "Mr. Kassan says if my report is halfway decent, he'll pass me."

Mercy glowed with satisfaction. "So that's it. And your mom can help you in math. She *is* a math professor."

"I don't know." Now that I'd announced my dire situation, I felt vulnerable, exposed. I didn't want their charity—as much as I needed it.

"Here's the way it's gonna be," Mercy declared. "We're

gonna boost you up. You're gonna pass. Or"—she hesitated a fraction of a second—"I'll have my nose ring
removed. That's how sure I am."

It was the first time I'd laughed out loud in months.
"You'd never do that, Merce. It took forever to convince
your parents to let you have it. You love that ring."

"That's why you have no choice but to pass," she
pointed out to me.

❧

"Why aren't we going to Jasmine's house?" Rex complained. "I wanted to hang out with them."

"I can't watch a fashion show," I snapped.

"Why not?" the dog prompted.

"I don't want to," I whispered, so as not to attract
attention in the crowded mall. We were on our way to
meet Regan.

"Because it might be fun?" he prodded.

What's the command for shut up? I thought, too tired
to engage.

"Well, I'm proud of you anyway," Rex said.

"For what?"

"Letting your friends help."

"They offered," I corrected him. "I haven't decided
yet."

"Have you decided to repeat eighth grade, then?"

·· 124 ··

Who knew a dog could be so annoying? "Rex, mind your own business." I took a water bottle out of my bag and tossed it on the floor. "Get it! Give it!" I commanded.

I swear Rex rolled his eyes at me.

"One thing you should know, though," he said as he dropped the bottle by my feet. "The reason Jasmine is doing so well in French is that she's getting her test answers off the Internet. It's how she's gotten through the whole semester."

Très bien pour elle. Good for her, I thought.

But I didn't mean it.

·· 14 ··

Hoots and Boots

By the end of May, we'd completed eight weeks of training. All our dogs, even the doggedly dumb Romeo and vertically stunted Sir Sniffs-a-Lot, Clark Kent, had come a long way. Most had learned to heel, lead a blind person, stop at curbs, retrieve anything we asked for, help someone in a wheelchair get dressed, push elevator and automatic door buttons, and flip light switches. Daffodil and Rex even mastered the ins and outs of a revolving door. I know *people* who have trouble with that!

There were four weeks of lessons to go. Then LuLu would administer the Public Access Test. The dogs who passed would meet the recipients—the disabled people—they'd be paired with, go home with. That was a detail I totally refused to think about.

When Rex and I showed up for our Monday class, JJ Pico had returned. After he'd skipped the field trip to the mall and a few classes after that, I thought maybe he'd dropped out.

JJ deliberately didn't look my way, but I kept him in my crosshairs. He found a seat at the far end of the row, crossed his arms, slouched, and stretched out his legs. If he was trying for cool, casual, and comfortable, he missed by a leg—specifically, the one he couldn't keep still. It was bouncing and shaking. He was uncomfortable? Nervous?

Good.

"They've got some catching up to do. But if we all pitch in, I'm betting we can bring Otis up to speed." LuLu had been talking. It was something about devoting extra time to help out the truants.

Overtime with JJ and Otis?

Trey, Clark Kent's trainer, raised his arm. "Sorry, but I can't stay late to help. My schedule is really packed."

What he said. 'Cause no way was I aiding and abetting a known liar. Why had he even bothered to come back? No one wanted him here. Well, maybe Lissa, his at-risk buddy.

"Isn't it great that JJ's back? You have another chance to get the truth out of him!" And Rex. His excited barks echoed off the walls.

LuLu was on to today's lesson, which she termed "the bootie class."

In dog training class, bootie means . . . little boots.

She distributed packets containing four paw-sized bright red booties with pebbled rubber soles, mesh uppers, and velcro straps. Megan and Maria, trainers of Romeo and Daffodil, cooed, "These are so cute!" while Clark Kent's Trey and Chainsaw's Lissa grumbled, "These are ridiculous." Two people didn't react: me and JJ.

"These are your Bark'n Boots," LuLu told us. "They may look a little undignified, but they serve an important purpose for a service dog. Can anyone guess what that is?"

Nothing besides "dumb fashion accessory" came to mind.

Maria had a thought. "To protect them from the scorching heat of the sidewalk?"

"Excellent guess." LuLu gave her props. "That's one reason."

"But their paws are padded. Isn't that enough?" Trey wondered.

"You're right, and for most dogs, most of the time, that *would* be enough. But what if your dog goes to live with someone in a city, and has to spend long stretches on that hot sidewalk? Or your dog may end up in a snowy climate—ice gets caught in the pockets between the pads. That's very painful for a dog. Ice can also be slippery, so the bottoms of the booties have deep grooves, like a tire. Anytime the dog has to be on rough terrain, the rubber soles give them traction, helps keep them—and their partner—upright."

"What about sand?" I surprised myself by joining the conversation. "People take dogs to the beach."

"Grains of sand can be irritating," LuLu agreed. "When the dog is working at a beach, the booties should be worn at least some of the time."

Another tidbit: dogs sweat through their paws, so they shouldn't spend long stretches of time in the booties.

Our goal for today was to get the dogs comfortable in their booties, not to struggle when their owners put them on; to be able to walk naturally in them.

Mission: not easily accomplished.

But it *was* a hoot. In the old days, I'd have texted pictures to Mercy, Jasmine, and Kendra—I kind of wanted to now, but the sound of my laughter was strange to my ears. And I was laughing hard. We all were.

None of the dogs, not even Rex, adapted easily to paw coverings. Clark Kent worked at biting his off, and Romeo refused to stand once Megan got them on him. Otis was traumatized. He kept them on, but no amount of cajoling could get the petrified poodle to proceed forward.

The rest, Rex, Daffodil, and Chainsaw, acted like they'd stepped in a sticky oil spill and were trying to extract themselves, one paw at a time. They obeyed our "let's go" command but looked like clumsy newborn colts, tripping all over themselves, unable to get their footing. They danced, they hopped, they wobbled, they teetered and tottered, their paws flailed out sideways. They'd raise one paw at a time really high in the air, then clomp it down hard. It was almost as if they were deliberately trying to be funny: a YouTube moment if ever there was one.

For the first time in months, I laughed so hard, I felt real tears.

When I saw JJ smiling, I shut down.

Neither of us should have been having fun.

And I shouldn't be forced into helping him catch up—no one should.

After class, I said as much to LuLu. Not that I expected her to change her mind. Our leader had a ton of great qualities, but flexibility wasn't one of them. Her response, however, unnerved me. "If JJ were any other kid, I'd agree with you. No one should be able to skip all those classes, return, and expect everyone to scramble so he can get caught up."

"Why the exception for him?" I said warily.

"A request came from the juvenile division of the West Palm Police, asking that we admit Mr. Pico and his dog to the program and give him special attention if he needed it."

"Who on the squad told you that?" I asked.

She looked momentarily confused. "I thought *you'd* know."

I reddened. "I don't know what you're talking about."

"In that case," she said delicately, "you might want to ask someone in your family."

I might not. Because if she was implying that my *dad* had placed JJ in this program, that would mean they knew each other well. That my dad had worked with him. And even if my mom had mentioned the possibility, even if Rex had gushed, "He worshipped your dad," it still couldn't be true.

∾

Grudgingly, I benched the JJ situation, at least temporarily. I had to focus on facts, formulas, and French idioms. After school, on the days I didn't have canine training, I went for brain training. Tutoring, that is. Mercy and I met at the library, where she was determined to pound enough world culture into me that I'd pass the final. Since I'd stopped paying attention, the class had covered three units: Africa, the Middle East, and Southeast Asia. I'd been mentally MIA for all of it. Even now, I couldn't drum up a lot of interest. Used to be, I'd find a creative way to make even the most boring subject palatable—boring, as in Russian Revolution snooze-inducing—and pull off As.

Now I could only hope my ability to memorize stuff hadn't abandoned me.

I got lucky. With Mercy as a tutor, and my own rusty, yet still functioning skills, by the end of our first week, I felt a glimmer of hope. Maybe I wouldn't fail everything.

Mercy confessed relief. No way did she want to remove her nose ring.

By the second week, it looked like I was going to be okay in social studies and science. And maybe language arts. Though *The Pigman & Me* wasn't too interesting, at least I finished it.

As for the dreaded algebra, I struggled on my own. Math professor Mom was clueless about the rank school situation, and I hoped to keep it that way. I let her think I was just hanging out with Mercy and the girls after school. It was nice to see the hope in Mom's eyes. Maybe one day it wouldn't be a total lie.

Then there was French. Jasmine's idea of tutoring was simple yet effective. She simply handed me the answers to the homework assignments, which I copied, and effectively got credit.

Jazz had a knack for knowing when pop quizzes were about to happen, and supplied me with those answers, too. I didn't ask questions. Just because Rex-the-talking-dog said she was cheating didn't make it true.

Doubt nagged at me, especially when one day in the middle of class, Jasmine was summoned to the guidance counselor's office. A session with Ms. Downy was never a good thing, even when it didn't involve talk therapy or grief counseling.

"Be right back," she mouthed to me and Kendra.

She didn't return that period, or the next.

·· 15 ··

Confessions

That night, I was lolling belly-down on my bed with the French textbook open in front of me. I hadn't gotten any notes from Jasmine today, so I tried catching up on my own. Diligently, I conjugated: *je connais; vous connaissez; nous connaissons*—I know, you know, we know. Suddenly, a shot of hot stinky dog breath polluted my space.

Rex's snowy paws inched up on the edge of the bedspread. "Wanna play?" the irrepressible pooch panted in anticipation.

"Can't," I said, motioning at the homework.

"But wait till you see what I found!" Rex's paws momentarily disappeared. A minute later, the whole bed shook as his bulky body bounced on it. He'd brought a gift: my old catcher's mitt.

I frowned. "Where'd you get that?"

"Your closet. BTW, it's a worse wreck than your room."

"You shouldn't be snooping in there," I scolded him.

"I found a softball, too."

"Good for you. Pretend they're chew toys—chomp and destroy." I tossed the mitt on the floor.

"Ah, come on," he urged. "Let's have a catch for old time's sake."

Old time's sake? He'd been here less than three months—we don't have old times. Besides, I will never wear that glove again.

"There's still enough light outside," Rex continued. "We could play for a while; then you can get back to your homework."

Le chien parle. The dog talks. *Le chien parle trop!* The dog talks too much!

Rex rested his wiry snout right on the open text-book and stared at me with big hopeful eyes. If I looked hard enough, I mused, would I see a soul in there? I reached over and with my thumb, smoothed the spot between his eyes. "Who are you, Rex?" I whispered.

"Who am I? I'm the guy you saved from the pound! I'm the luckiest dog in the whole world!"

"But what are you, really?"

"What do you mean?" Rex looked perplexed.

"Talking dogs don't exist. So what else is there I need to know?"

"Hmmm . . . You already know my taste in haute cuisine . . ."

I bent forward at the waist and cradled his head in my hands. "Do I need to see a shrink?" I shuddered at the thought.

"About what?"

"About you! You're like a drug-sniffing dog, except you somehow know when people are cheating or stealing. Detectives, private investigators do that, not untrained shelter dogs."

"I'm *ruff* on crime!" he chortled.

I groaned.

"Oh, come on, Stacey, where's your sense of humor? That was funny!"

"Rex . . . if you really want to help me, make me understand what's going on. 'Cause I'm really confused."

"Would you believe I'm Deputy Dawg?"

I stared at him.

"What do I have to do to get a smile out of you?"

"Tell me why you purposely led me to that boy's house."

"Can't we just play catch?"

"Why is that so important to you?" I demanded.

Rex looked genuinely puzzled. "You're overthinking

it. You're a girl, I'm a dog. You throw the ball, I run after it and bring it back. What's the problem?"

"The problem? The problem is that . . . ," I sputtered, then gave up. What am I doing? What am I thinking?

Rex stretched, got up on all fours, and jumped off the bed. A second later, the softball was in his mouth. He sat ramrod straight and stared at me. The dog had a one-track mind. He wanted to play ball. He'd wait.

"Fine!" I grumbled. I closed the textbook, swung my legs over the side of the bed, and plucked the ball out of his mouth. "You win—go get it!" I reared back and hurled the ball across the room—it bounced hard off the wall, chipping the black paint.

Rex dashed after it, cheering. "Now you're talking!"

"You're talking." My sister, never one for subtlety, let alone knocking, slipped inside the door just as Rex caught up with the softball.

I shrugged. "I'm playing with the dog."

"I heard you," she contradicted. "You were having a conversation with the dog. Like he's real."

"Of course he's real, Regan. Does he look stuffed to you?"

She eyed him critically. "He could use some exercise."

"So I've put on a few pounds!" Miffed, Rex dropped the ball.

"Why's he barking at me?" Regan asked.

He's not barking at you. He's talking to me. You insulted him.

"What do you want, Regan?"

She didn't answer. Instead, she picked up the softball. "Ick. He drooled on it." She grabbed a T-shirt from the floor and wiped it off.

"Seriously, Regan. What favor do you need?"

"Like I only talk to you when I need something?" She tossed her hair over her shoulder regally. *A move I couldn't pull off if I tried.*

I folded my arms and gave her an accusatory stare.

She avoided my gaze. Her eyes darted around the room until they fell on the catcher's mitt, which had landed haphazardly atop a pile of clothes. "It's good you're playing with that again."

"Don't remember asking your opinion."

With a humongous sigh, she dropped into the chair by my desk, still toying with the ball. Her manicured nails, a neon pink, looked incongruous around the scuffed, grayish white softball. Then she really shocked me— she tossed it at me. Instinctively, I shielded my face. Her throw went sailing over my head. I reached up to grab it before it smashed into the trophies on the shelf above my bed.

"Oopsie," she said with a giggle. "I never did have great aim."

"Only with a put-down," I said.

Suddenly, she laughed. "Remember when Dad tried to teach me to play?"

In spite of myself, I smiled. How could I forget? I was about six; Regan, nine. I'd just started peewee league. We were in the backyard and Dad was pitching as I practiced my meager swings. Regan flounced outside wearing flip-flops and a frilly pink sundress. Dad wanted her to join us, but Regan, flaxen-haired, pouty, and adorable, didn't want to. Somehow, he talked her into staying for one at bat. "All you have to do is aim the ball at Gracie's bat. When she hits it, catch it and throw it back to her. It's fun, you'll see."

He positioned Regan a few feet from me. Even so, her wimpy toss landed short.

"You throw like a girl!" I teased, pleased to be better at something than my big sister.

Regan trumped me: she always did. "That's because I *am* a girl, you freak."

Catching the shattered look on my face, my dad intervened, assuring me that playing sports didn't make me any less feminine than my sister. Even so, watching Regan sashay away, my budding self-esteem had taken a direct hit.

"Ow—watch where you're throwing," she said now, as I underhanded the ball back at her. "I almost broke a nail."

"And on that note, I ask again: What do you want, Regan?"

My sister is not shy. She doesn't do avoidance. So it surprised me when, instead of just telling me, she slipped off the chair onto the carpet and busied herself with the mess on the floor. "This needs to be washed," she said of my denim cutoffs. "But this monstrosity"—she held my moth-eaten Marlins T-shirt at arm's length like it might contaminate her—"this goes in the garbage. As do these." She plucked a pair of smelly sneakers up by the laces and dumped them on top of the T-shirt.

"I like those!" I protested but made no move to stop her. The only time my sister stoops to cleaning up my stuff is when she's nervous. Really nervous.

I watched as she sat cross-legged on the floor and organized my trash heap. After she'd made neat piles of the clothes, she rounded up the random photos that littered the carpet, squared off their corners until she had one neat deck. "Do you have an album to put them in?" she asked.

I tossed her an empty shoebox from my closet. I'd wait her out—and get a semi-decluttered room in the bargain. I looked at the stuff she'd designated "garbage" and realized there was more that could go. I rounded up the softball trophies and went to put them in the pile.

That stopped Regan. "No. You'll regret that," she said, pulling them away from me.

I'd had enough. "Okay, Regan, spit it out. Why are you here?"

She focused on something over my shoulder. "Sheena kind of admitted the thing with Mom's jewelry."

My eyebrows shot up. So Regan was there to apologize? That's why she was cleaning my room?

"Anyway." She took a dramatic breath. "Here's the thing. I knew . . . that is, I suspected, that every once in a while, she might have lifted something. But from a *store*. Not from someone's *home*."

"That makes it okay?"

"I guess I always told myself it was her thing. If it didn't affect me—"

"*A chacun à son goût?*" The French phrase popped into my head and out my mouth.

"Huh?" My sister, who had enough trouble with her native tongue, wisely skipped taking foreign languages in high school.

"It's French. It means, 'Each to her own.' Sort of, 'live and let live.'"

"I didn't think she'd ever steal from *my* house," Regan croaked. "I feel so betrayed." Her face crumpled. Big round anime-sized tears drizzled down her cheek.

I didn't know what to say. I'd never had to comfort Regan before.

"I trusted her," she sobbed. "I'm so stupid!"

"You're not stupid, Regan." It was the best I could

do. I scrounged up a box of tissues from the night table and handed it to her. I should have felt vindicated. Instead, watching my sister fall apart, my heart ached.

"Did you tell Mom?" I asked gently.

She shook her head and blew her nose noisily. "I'm too embarrassed."

I didn't know my sister could be embarrassed. But I completely related.

"So anyway," she continued. "I told Sheena I'm done, not to call or text or anything. And don't dare show up here again." Her voice caught, and she dabbed at her eyes.

"You iced your BFF?" That was huge. Bigger, maybe, than the stealing thing. "What'd she say?"

"You know." Regan waved her hand dismissively. "Tried to make excuses, said she had a disease! Can you believe her nerve? She promised to get help if I forgave her."

"But you're not going to—?"

Regan shook her head. "She violated our family. That's unforgiveable. If you hadn't caught her—"

"It was really Rex." That came out of my mouth before I could stop it.

Regan snorted. "Maybe he should be a police dog instead of a service dog."

"About that . . . about Rex, I have something to ask

you," I ventured. "You said Dad suggested training a service dog."

"He did," she confirmed, wiping away her tears. "Okay, maybe he was kidding when he said it would look good for my college application."

"Did he know specifically about Canine Connections?" I asked.

"Of course. How do you think I came up with them?"

I guess "research" was out of the question.

"Do you know if—"

"What?"

"Did he ever, you know, have any of the at-risk kids train a dog, like as a life-lesson thing—to learn responsibility, empathy, helping someone worse off than yourself?"

"All the time." Regan looked at me curiously. "I thought you knew that, and that the real reason you didn't force me into doing it was because you wanted to continue Dad's work."

Her words hit me like a punch. I'd never thought about it like that. Guess I was the only one, because Mom knew about Dad's involvement in the program. We shared a lot of stuff, me and my dad, but when I think about it, I realize it was always my stuff, whatever I was going through, or interested in. He never talked about his work. Not specifically. Had I ever asked? Had Regan? Is that why she knew about this?

For a fleeting second, I saw my sister differently. True, she'll always be everything I'm not, inside out and outside in. Outside our house, what Regan is—beautiful, popular, extroverted, trendy—is valued. She's the girl other girls wish they were.

No one, as far as I know, wishes she were me.

Inside our house, my dad made me feel like the special one. I always thought he valued the person I was over Regan. But as the days go by, I can't get away from the feeling—the knowing—that my dad was okay with both of us. That he loved her as deeply as he loved me.

"Regan?"

"What?"

"Would it be okay if I helped with your college essay?"

She narrowed her still-moist eyes. "What makes you think it needs help?"

I fessed up. "You got a lot of it wrong—about the training, I mean."

A real smile formed on her bow lips. A warm smile, a sisterly smile.

An "I win again!" smile.

·· 16 ··

A Wheel Scare

Dealing with homework, getting tutored, and actually paying attention in school left fewer brain cells devoted to obsessing about JJ. But whenever I did see him, the righteous anger in me fired up again. I counted six miserable times since he'd returned to Canine Connections with at least that many more to go. Worse was feeling pushed in one direction, pulled in another.

Rex pushed me to use class time to "get the truth out of him."

The force of my fury pulled me farther away from him.

I dreaded what was coming next: my turn to work one-on-one with him. So far, LuLu and the others had taken turns helping JJ and Otis catch up.

On the last Friday in May, it was my turn.

I refused. On the grounds that I hated him.

"You're not doing it for him," LuLu reminded me. "Otis is a smart dog, and he has a good chance of passing the Public Access Test. He could give a disabled person a chance at an independent life. That's our goal here."

Hard to argue with that. But I found a way. "I have nothing against the dog. I'll take him home for the weekend. Rex and I will work with him."

I thought that was a brilliant compromise, but not so much. "Grace." Lulu gave my shoulder a light squeeze. "That's very generous of you, but you know there's more to it. JJ's participation in this program is crucial. Otherwise, he may end up in a juvenile facility."

"Works for me."

"Our job is to help him avoid that," she said gently.

"I can't be around him." I folded my arms defensively. "Do you know how it even feels to see him in class?"

"I'm sure it's been hard," she said sympathetically. "Yet in spite of it, you and Rex are my shining stars. That says a lot about your character."

I scowled.

She continued. "Everyone who's worked with JJ says he's a quick study, cooperative, no attitude. And I need you only a few hours on Sunday. I promise it'll be in a public place. You won't be alone with him."

I pouted. Making me work with JJ was beyond unfair.

Rex, who had his own agenda, went straight for my weak spot. "It's probably what your father would have wanted."

I pointed a warning finger at the dog. "Don't go there, Rex!"

I ignored LuLu's bewilderment.

"I'm just sayin' *if* your old man got this kid into the program, he probably wanted him to succeed."

∾

At least LuLu was true to her word. I did end up in a public place with JJ. Late Sunday morning, she met us in the parking lot of a CVS superstore in Jupiter. My mission was to help teach Otis to focus and function in a big, busy store. The lesson was like the one in the Gardens Mall and one we did in a grocery store, with one major adjustment: this time, we'd be in wheelchairs. We'd find out what it was really like to rely on a dog to help us shop.

LuLu provided wheelchairs and basic instruction in their use. "Remember, you can't get out of the chair; your mobility is limited," were her parting words.

If not for being stuck with JJ, I would've been psyched by the assignment, a real test for Rex and me. The only way to get through it was to focus on Otis, act like JJ wasn't even there.

It wasn't a viable plan. The dogs stayed close to each other—and they were strapped to our chairs by their leashes.

"Heel!" I told Rex.

Obediently, he positioned himself next to the wheelchair.

JJ mimicked me. Only one problem. The dog is supposed to be on your left and Otis was on JJ's right. When that happens, you're to say, "Side," signaling the dog to walk around the chair. JJ didn't know this. I could have not said anything, let him do it wrong. But the words were out of my mouth before I could debate it. "You need to tell him, 'Side.' He should be on your left."

When Otis obeyed, I said stiffly, "You should praise him for doing the right thing."

"Good boy," he told Otis agreeably. He turned to me, his leg jangling. "So what do we do now?"

"We start." I wheeled into the store through the automatic doors and pointed at the stack of small shopping baskets by the entrance. "Look," I instructed Rex. When he focused on them, I said, "Bring it to me."

The task wasn't hard for Rex, who gingerly grasped the edge of the top basket with his teeth, lifted it out, and placed it on my lap.

"Whoa." That was JJ. "Dude, your dog is amazing.

It's like he's human or something. I don't think this one can do that." He flicked his eyes at Otis.

"If you'd been at the classes where we practiced, he might have a better shot," I said.

He shrugged.

I rolled my eyes.

Rex barked.

Otis, confused, sat down.

"Get his attention," I said. "Then point at what you want and say, 'Look.'"

At the sound of JJ's voice, Otis got up. He seemed to understand but wasn't as agile as Rex, and this was his first try at the task. He used his paws instead of his teeth, and knocked the whole stack over. Instantly, a customer who'd been watching us intervened. "I'll help," she offered, straightening the stack and placing a basket on JJ's lap. He gave her a thankful grin.

I grimaced. We'd been taught that when the dog makes a mistake, you're supposed to correct him, give him another chance. But this was probably a tough start for JJ and Otis, so I didn't criticize him.

Next up: buying toothpaste, soap, aspirin, and shaving cream. When you can walk, you don't think twice about shopping. When you're in a wheelchair with a dog at your side, you become wider and the aisles suddenly seem narrow.

I went in front of JJ and stopped by the toothpaste.

The idea was to pick one on a high shelf, and get the dog to bring it to you. I chose a tube of something that promised super whitening, then lined up the wheelchair and dog as close to it as possible. "Get it," I said, pointing out the toothpaste I wanted. Rex dutifully got up on his hind legs and after several tries, managed to knock the right one to the floor, pick it up, and put it in the basket.

"Good job!" I praised him.

JJ's eyes were wide.

"Tag, you're it. Show Otis what you want."

"This is weird, man," he said. "I don't like it."

Honestly? I'd thought this was a cool assignment, but now that we were doing it, I agreed with him. It was hard! Worse, the looks of pity we were getting from the other shoppers reminded me too sharply of the way the kids at school looked at me right after Dad died. I hated it.

I also hated that I was stuck here, at least until we finished shopping. I determined to get through it quickly.

Rex did his part by helping Otis. At least I think that's what my dog was doing. I'll say this for the poodle. He didn't get distracted by other customers, even when a kid came over to pet him. He looked at JJ for guidance. To his credit, he followed my lead.

Mostly, they did all right. Otis made a mess of the aspirin shelves, but retrieved the shaving cream and soap without too much collateral damage. And although he tried to mask it, JJ couldn't hide the look of pride on his face.

We finished our shopping and it was time to pay. Rex and I had practiced this before. I demonstrated how to get the dog to pull the credit card out of your pocket, then give it to the cashier.

Rex performed with his usual panache, paws atop the counter, watching as the cashier scanned the card and returned it. Rex gingerly took it and dropped it, and the bagged items, in my shopping basket.

JJ and Otis were next. A line had formed behind him. When Otis didn't retrieve the credit card from his pocket right away, JJ cheated—he pulled it out and gave it to him. Which is completely unhelpful if Otis ends up with someone without use of his hands.

I didn't bother pointing that out. JJ had started to sweat as the line behind us got longer. I could see he was itching to get out of the chair and pay the normal way.

"Rex"—I leaned over the side of the chair and whispered to my dog—"show Otis how to give the card to the cashier."

"I'm not supposed to," he demurred, "but I'll do it for you, Tracey."

As we headed out to the parking lot to wait for

LuLu, JJ asked, "What if you don't have a credit card? How does the dog pay in cash?"

"You put the approximate amount you need in your wallet. The dog gives the wallet to the cashier."

"How do you know the kid at the register isn't going to take a few extra bucks for himself?" JJ queried.

"You don't. Sometimes you just have to trust that people are honorable. That they'll do the right thing." *Unlike you,* I thought. "But it's true that disabled people are vulnerable, easy targets sometimes. Which really stinks."

On the sidewalk outside the store, JJ stood up and folded the wheelchair. "I'm done with this contraption."

"You're lucky you can," I said obnoxiously— deliberately staying put.

JJ's cell phone rang just then. I wasn't trying to listen but couldn't help overhearing him tell someone our location. "I'm getting a ride home," he said to me when the call was over.

Like I cared. Unless of course it was the gang coming to get him. Then I cared very much. If LuLu didn't show soon, I would call her.

Without a training exercise, JJ and I didn't have anything to say to each other. Fine by me. He seemed jumpy, though, rubbing his palms together, shifting on his feet. Then he nodded toward his left. "There's a vending machine around the corner. I'm getting a soda. You want something?"

A cold bottle of water would be good. But not from him. An idea popped into my head. "Come on, Rex," I said, propelling myself in front of JJ, along the sidewalk until we rounded the corner. JJ and Otis followed. When we reached the vending machine, I said, "Might as well have Rex do it. Technically, we're still working."

JJ shot me an "are you nuts?" look. But I could tell he was impressed as Rex and I worked it. The dog pushed the correct button with his nose, retrieved the bottle of water when it landed in the basket.

"Why don't you try with Otis?" I said. To make room for him, I backed the wheelchair off the curb, into the parking lot.

"I've had enough," he said, depositing the coins in the slot. He kept his eyes on the soda can as it plunked into the catchall. "Just to get this straight, it doesn't thrill me to be around you, either."

At first, I didn't get what he was talking about. As soon as I did, I nearly choked on my drink. "Excuse me?" I said, mopping my face with the back of my hand.

"I blew off those classes after . . . what happened."

I started to boil. "By 'what happened,' you mean the night I got lost in your neighborhood and caught you in a lie? After your friends blurted that your brother is in jail? You were in that car all along and know exactly what went down. Is *that* what you mean?"

He flushed; sweat beads had collected on his forehead and he looked away.

I went on ranting. "You didn't want to see me because you felt guilty—"

"And remorseful," Rex cut in. "Now would be a good moment to ask him."

"Ask him?"

JJ's thick brow furrowed. Uh-oh, had I said that out loud? I coughed to cover up my embarrassment, and heard myself say stiffly, "So obviously, you knew my father."

"You didn't know that? Dude's the only reason I'm here." He took a gulp of soda.

So that was it. Confirmation. As if I still needed it.

Angry as I was, my voice came out whiny. "My dad worked with you. He tried to help you. Shooting him— that's how you repaid him?"

JJ's hands went up so fast, his soda can slipped to the ground. "Whoa. Chill. I didn't shoot anybody."

"But you know who did." My heart started to pound.

He bent over to pick up the Pepsi. "It wasn't supposed to go down like that. He wasn't supposed to . . ."

JJ didn't get a chance to finish the sentence. Neither of us saw the car coming, or even heard the blaring beat of the radio, until it was too late. The stealth shove came from behind me—the fender of the car smacked against the back of the wheelchair with enough force to flip it over and send it crashing to the ground. I felt myself toppling over as the dogs barked frantically. Through it all, I heard JJ's panicked cries. "Stop it! No! Stop!"

I tried to break my fall with my hands. Still, I did a face-plant into the hot pavement. Instantly, Rex's wet nose was in my face, and though it sounded like frenzied barking, his doggy voice was in my ear. "Are you okay? I'm so sorry! I tried to warn you! Oh, please, Macey, tell me you're okay!"

JJ quickly pulled the chair off me and helped me to my feet. "You hurt?" he asked anxiously. His expression was total shock—and fear.

Menacing laughter came from the car.

I brushed myself off. I'd skinned my palms and knees, and probably scratched my face, but luckily, I was in one piece. Rex pressed his trembling body against my leg. "Can you stand? Is anything broken? I wanted to warn you—"

I stroked his wiry head. "I'm fine, it's okay."

JJ turned furiously to the driver of the car. "What the hell, man—what's the matter with you? You could've hurt her."

"Down, bro—it was just a tap."

I wasn't surprised, but still, a chill went through my sweaty body as I identified the perps. Hector and Chris. Fear prickled up my spine like a skittering spider. Unsteadily, I pulled away from JJ and took a step toward them.

"Uh-oh, I think she's gonna spit on me again. I'm really scared," Hector heckled me. As if by some secret dog sign, Rex and Otis lunged at the open window of the car together, a tag team of teeth-baring terror. Before Hector could retract his arm, Rex had a juicy elbow in his jaw.

"Rex, no!" I cried. I wanted to do more than spit at them myself, but I couldn't let Rex bite. I'd heard too many stories of dogs being put down for attacking people, no matter what the reason.

Luckily, the demonstration of canine ferocity scared them, or more likely, they didn't want to attract any more attention to themselves. Panic edged into their voices. "JJ! Get in the car! Now!"

JJ looked torn, appalled even.

Not enough to turn his back on them, though. He took a reluctant step away from me.

I grabbed his arm. "Wait."

"I can't, man, I gotta go," he said nervously.

"You said it wasn't supposed to happen. With my dad . . ." I sounded desperate. I felt desperate. JJ shook my hand off him. It was too late. Whatever he'd planned to tell me was lost. He stepped off the curb, toward the car. Then swiftly, over his shoulder, he said—just loud enough so I could hear, but the boys in the car couldn't—"The Jupiter Pier. Eight tonight."

· · 17 · ·

Secrets in the Sand

Foamy white-tipped waves lapped at the slick rocks surrounding the Jupiter Pier, a narrow stretch of board-walk poking out into the ocean. During the day, ama-teur fishermen stood elbow to elbow, buckets of bait at their feet, casting lines into the water, in the hopes of snagging a sunfish or maybe a snapper.

At night, it was deserted.

The pier itself bisected a beach. North of it was a leafy public park, dotted with campsites, well-marked trails, and picnic tables. South of it, one of the few wide sand beaches in Jupiter to boast a lifeguard. The area was a popular gathering spot for families, retirees, and keg parties. That last one I only guessed at. I'd never been there without my family.

Until now. I was making what was either the

dumbest move of my life, or the one that'd give me the answers I was desperate to have. Maybe both. I hedged my bets by bringing Rex along. I was scared, but not entirely stupid.

I'd told Mom and Regan I was going to the movies with my friends and had Regan drop me at a shopping center with an eighteen-screen multiplex. From there, it was only a short walk to the beach.

It wasn't supposed to go down like that. He wasn't supposed to . . . Ever since he'd said it earlier that day, JJ's cut-short admission had played round and round in my head on a loop.

Die. That's what he'd meant. My dad wasn't supposed to die. That was the end of the sentence, the beginning of the truth.

How much would JJ tell me now? Was I ready to hear it? Could I bear hearing it? And what if JJ had set me up, only to lie to me again?

I actually knew little about him. Just that he lived in a run-down neighborhood and hung out with really bad kids, kids who carried guns and were probably gang members. I wouldn't be surprised if JJ had an arrest record all his own. That's why he was "at-risk." At risk for juvenile detention now, maybe worse when he grew up. When would that be? JJ looked like a high school kid, but I had no idea how old he really was.

I had to accept this, too: JJ Pico was in Canine Connections because my dad had placed him there.

Was that enough to trust that I wasn't walking into a trap worse than another lie? That he wouldn't bring his perp-posse along to ambush me again? I couldn't know until he showed up. My own words came back to me: "Sometimes you just have to trust that people are honorable, that they'll do the right thing."

For whatever it was worth, Rex had no qualms about going. Just the opposite. "I get to go to the beach! I can roll in the sand and run into the water! Thank you for taking me!"

"We'll be here only a short while," I reminded him, and checked the time. It was just past eight. I'd been here twenty minutes, standing under a streetlamp about halfway down the pier. My stomach was in a hundred knots.

Rex heard them before I saw them.

"It's Otis!" he cheered, straining on the leash toward the darkened park.

"I don't see anything." I squinted.

"It's his scent," Rex said, his tail wagging a mile a minute. "A soft bouquet of bougainvillea stirred into bouillabaisse. I'd know him anywhere."

Just then two figures emerged from the tree-shrouded park onto the lighted pier. JJ was wheeling a bike, Otis trotted beside him. I listened for other noises, specifically, a car that might've followed him, but I heard nothing except the splash of the waves.

As he approached, I noticed he was in the same clothes as earlier, lowrider jeans, unbuttoned long-sleeved flannel over a T-shirt, unlaced sneakers. Yet in the diffused light cast by the streetlamp, he looked tougher somehow, borderline sinister. At that moment, I wished I'd worn something more substantial than flip-flops and one of Regan's cute shorts outfits. I felt at a disadvantage.

"Hey," JJ said as he leaned his bike against the pier's metal railing. "You showed."

"Did you come alone?" I asked anxiously.

He nodded, shoving his hands into his jeans pockets sheepishly. "I'm sorry about what happened before, in the parking lot. That really blew."

"Those thugs aren't picking you up or anything?" I was still suspicious.

"If they even knew I was here, I'd be toast," he said.

I'd have felt better if I believed him.

Rex and Otis had greeted each other by leaping up and smacking paws, a doggy version of a high-five. They barked and circled each other playfully. As soon as we let them off their leashes, they ducked under the railing and scampered down the short embankment to the beach.

"Rex, no—come back!" I shouted.

"Let 'em run," JJ said. "We can't miss them with their glow-in-the-dark vests."

True, but I wanted Rex with me. I suggested we walk down the beach after them. We wouldn't go far. I only needed JJ to finish what he'd started to say. Then I'd grab Rex and split.

We knelt, grasped the metal railing, twisted around, and scooched under it. JJ went first, sure-footed down the rocks and onto the sand. He offered me his hand, but I refused. I could manage the rocky descent on my own, even in flip-flops. Of course I skidded and landed on my butt. Which was now soaked from the slimy seaweed-covered rocks. How I'd explain that to my sister I didn't know. To JJ's credit, he didn't even snicker, just made sure I was okay—for the second time that day.

We walked in silence, accompanied only by a scattering of seagulls hoping to pick up a stray crumb. The wet, densely packed sand crunched beneath our feet. Finally, JJ said, "If it makes a difference, it wasn't you they wanted to hurt."

"What were they aiming for? The soda machine?"

"It was a message to me," JJ said. "They don't like me hanging out with you."

"We are *not* hanging out," I contradicted him.

"I know, but they don't see it like that. They see me with you—or around you—and it's not cool."

My snarky side eclipsed my fear. "So they decide to run me over?"

JJ apparently felt the need to defend his cohorts, or maybe just explain them. "Hector and Chris, they're my brother's friends—"

"So that makes them your friends, too?" I challenged. To my horror, a little voice in my head chirped, *He's not like them. He's better than they are.* I kicked the sand, as if to kick the voice away.

"It's not like that . . . exactly. To them, they're letting me take my brother's place. They think I should feel honored. Not do anything to screw that up."

Being seen with me, he meant. Hanging out with the cop's kid—the cop they killed—would qualify as screwing up JJ's gang-trainee status. Which he should be honored to have. I felt sick, but all I said was, "Riiii-ght, the famous brother you claimed was in the car, but who's really in jail."

"I don't expect you to understand, but he used to protect me. Now that he's not around, I have to fend for myself."

"What do you mean?"

"Where I live it's either be cool with them, or be crushed by them. There's no in between. If you turn your back, there's nothing protecting you from them."

JJ had made his choice. *And now he's justifying it,*

that's why I'm here. He wants me to understand. Should I tell him now I never will?

JJ took my silence for disapproval, so he tried harder to explain. "I'm expected to take my brother's place while he's away. Hector, Chris, and those guys, they accept me. I'm part of something."

A gang. That's what you're part of. Just like your brother, and look where it landed him—in jail. I might have said it, too, but that annoying voice in my head intruded again. *He's a kid caught in a bad situation. Someone thought it was worth getting him out of it.*

I shouted the voice down. "You know what, JJ? I don't really care who you hang out with or why. I came here tonight so you could tell me what really happened the night my father got killed. You said it wasn't supposed to happen like that. Tell me what you know."

Just ahead, the dogs were frolicking without a care in the world, dashing into the tide, splashing, turning tail and racing back to the beach. Rex had his jaws around a rope of knotted seaweed and was trying to get Otis to play tug-of-war.

JJ stopped walking. "Is it okay if we sit?"

It wouldn't have been my first choice. The sand was moist and muddy from the receding tide, but my shorts were wet already. I planted myself a few feet away from him. The seagulls took this as a good sign, and took tentative steps toward us. JJ didn't seem to notice.

"Last summer, some guy's car got broken into—the cops pinned it on me."

"But you didn't do it," I recited sarcastically. All perps deny stuff.

He brushed me off. "It doesn't matter. It was a first offense. I was supposed to get off with probation. But instead I got Detective Abernathy."

My dad. *He's going to tell me*, I suddenly realized. *Not just about that night, but about everything.* I gestured for him to continue.

"He asked me a bunch of questions. He knew about my brother and Hector. He started coming round, checking on me and stuff. I stayed clean. Until one day I went for a ride with the guys. We had some open cans of beer, and I accidentally sideswiped another car."

"You were driving?"

"Yeah, and I'm fifteen. I don't have a permit. I got busted. My second offense."

"You were going to juvie," I concluded.

"Straight to," he said. "But then Detective Abernathy stepped in, told me I had a choice, something to try out—if it worked, I wouldn't have to go. He had a few kids that he worked with. Helped them stay out of trouble. If I wanted to try, I could avoid being locked up."

"What exactly did he do?" I asked, regretting that I knew so little about this part of Dad's life.

JJ picked up a shell and tossed into the ocean. I

couldn't help but notice: he used his left hand. "Detective A got us tutors for school, made sure we did our homework, stuff like that."

Stuff a parent would do, I thought with a start.

"He got a couple of kids part-time jobs. That's a big thing, 'cause it isn't easy to get hired when you, you know, have a record." He looked up to make sure I got the import of this. Then he leaned back on his elbows and stared out at the ocean. "He was kind of like this mentor, big brother, only not cheesy. He didn't just tell us stuff, he showed us that we were smart, and that we didn't have to end up in trouble all the time. We had a choice. But he didn't lecture us. He was cool that way. Joked around, took us to a basketball game one time, bought us lunch."

I couldn't help it, my heart swelled with pride. Then, as if I were on a roller coaster that'd just chugged to the highest point—it plunged. "So to thank him, you got him killed. Is that how it works?" I nearly choked on my words.

"It didn't happen like that. Like I said, he wasn't supposed to die."

Beads of sweat on his forehead and I noticed his foot jangling. "What *was* supposed to happen?" I asked.

He stuttered as he told me, bits and pieces at first, until the whole horrific story poured out.

"It was a Tuesday—two days before Thanksgiving.

I was heading to school, like usual, when Hector and Chris cruised by. They wanted me to hang out with them. I said I had school, but Hector laughed and told me to get in."

"You caved."

"It's not like I wanted to go," JJ said defensively. "But they got on my case bad, talking trash about how I thought I was better than them, now that I hang with a cop." JJ turned to me. "They meant Detective Abernathy."

Yeah, I'd figured that out.

"Said I turned into some police pansy, and wait till my brother found out. Then Chris threatened me, reminding me that Thomas wasn't around to protect me. So if I knew what was good for me, I'd man up, forget that school crap, and hang out with them."

I didn't know what to say. I had no idea what it was like to be bullied. Before I could push it away, I felt a twinge of empathy for him.

JJ continued. "So we were cruising, hanging out. In the afternoon, Hector said we were gonna pick up this other guy Tony. I only started to suspect something was up when we drove to the police precinct, circled the block, and parked a little ways away."

Whoa.

"I asked what we were doing there, but the guys blew me off. Then all of a sudden, Detective Abernathy comes out of the building. He's walking fast. I didn't think anyone would be stupid enough to follow a cop! Still . . ." JJ hung his head. "Just in case Detective A saw us, I slunk low in the seat."

"Front or back?" I asked, testing him.

"Back," he said.

This time, I believed him.

"Then I hear Chris say, 'He's early.'" JJ paused. "At that moment, everything happened so fast, I didn't understand. Only later, that's when I realized the whole thing was a setup."

"A setup?" I repeated dumbly.

"I didn't have time to even say anything. I saw a gun barrel flash. I tried to yell, but Tony clamped his hand over my mouth. 'Don't freak out, bro. We're just gonna give a little warning. The cop isn't welcome on our turf.'"

My mouth went dry. JJ kept talking,

"They waited until he got to his car. Tony said they were just going to shoot his tires out, mess up his day. That was the plan. But then someone stuck his arm out under the gun and jerked it upward. The shot went wild. Instead of hitting the tires or the windshield . . ." JJ trailed off. He didn't have to finish. We both knew how it ended. My heart was so heavy, I doubted I could ever get up. So I was shocked to hear myself blurt, "How could they shoot at a cop? Right by the precinct? How stupid could they be?"

"You don't understand," JJ said. "They think they're untouchable. That's the mentality."

For a long time after that, I couldn't speak. I cradled my head in my arms. My stomach heaved. I thought I might upchuck, right on the sand. But what came up wasn't the contents of my stomach—it was the burning need to get revenge. To cause as much harm and hurt as had been done to my family. "Who shot him? Who had the gun?" I demanded.

"I can't tell you that." JJ's voice was barely above a whisper.

"But you know," I said coldly.

"I told you this much because I really liked your old man. He helped me out a lot. And you're his kid. But I can't take it any further."

"You *have* to!" I exclaimed. "If you withhold information, that's a crime."

"So be it." With that, JJ jumped up and whistled for Otis.

"So be . . . nothing!" I shrieked, kicking the sand in frustration.

JJ's whistling brought Otis and Rex. My dog, sensing my distress, nuzzled close to me. I rested my head against his prickly muzzle and desperately tried to think of something to make JJ tell me the rest. He'd confessed this much because he was grateful to my dad. Worshipped him, Rex had said.

I looked up at JJ clipping the leash onto Otis's collar and quietly said, "If you don't go to the police and tell them what you told me—*and* who had the gun—it'll all have been for nothing. Everything my dad did for you. For nothing."

JJ lifted his chin. "I already said more than I should have. This is as far as I go."

"If you have an ounce of gratitude, the least you can do is honor his memory," I pressed on.

JJ's forehead crinkled. "Like make a donation or something?"

"Like remembering what he used to say." I could only hope my dad had given JJ the advice he'd imbued in me. " 'There's a time to be brave, and a time to cave—if you *know* something is the right thing to do, even if you're scared, do it anyway. Especially if you're scared.' "

By the light of the moon, I saw the color rise in JJ's face. I'd struck a nerve. I hammered away. "He would have wanted you to be brave."

"Not if it cost my life."

·· 18 ··

Magical Thinking

I stayed on the beach after JJ and Otis left, staring out into the ocean. It was mesmerizing. Thick stripes of moonbeams lit the surface of the water, illuminating the silhouette of a cruise ship far in the distance. I pictured my dad standing there, toes in the sand, taking in his favorite sight. He'd never get to feel this again.

But I would.

The thought had come out of nowhere and pounced on me like Rex in the morning. If a little part of Dad lived on in me, then maybe in some weird universe-righting-itself way, maybe he was seeing it, too. Something like hope welled up inside of me.

～

Later that night, I lay in bed trying to patch together what I'd just learned, and how much of it I believed.

If JJ had told the truth, the shooting had been planned all along—the time Dad left work didn't factor into it. They were waiting for him.

It never had anything to do with me.

Not guilty. That was my verdict. Maybe someday that would give me peace, but right now, at—I looked at the clock: 11:11 p.m.—the hole in my heart was every bit as big and jagged as the day we lost him.

The rest of it—they hadn't meant to shoot him, JJ was an innocent passenger with a conveniently vague memory—maybe was true, maybe not. It didn't matter. In JJ's world, gangs ruled. They took issue with a cop trying to help their friend's brother. In their twisted minds, Detective Abernathy had intruded on their turf, messed with one of their own. They couldn't let it be.

Their solution, to teach the cop and the kid a lesson, was carried out the only way they knew how, violently.

That they were only supposed to blow out my dad's tires, or smash his windshield, but hit him instead? They didn't care—worse, they didn't pay for it. Except for JJ's admission of being in the car, the police interrogation netted no solid evidence against any of them. No convictions, no indictments, no jail time. The conscience-less miscreants were home free.

Grand slam for them.

Torture for me and my family.

I wanted revenge. We deserved it. The West Palm Beach Police Force had not managed it for us. What were the chances a lone thirteen-year-old could get back at Hector, Chris, and that Tony guy? How could I inflict hurt, humiliation, and the kind of pain they'd caused us?

I wasn't exactly Wonder Woman, Xena, Nancy Drew, or that girl with the dragon tattoo.

So what *should* I do with this new info?

Tell someone, sure. But whom?

I suppose I could have told Regan, the first person I saw after meeting JJ. She'd picked me up at the shopping center, but as usual, had been deep in Regan-land, talking all about herself. She'd asked no questions, not even, what movie did you see, or where are your friends? Or why are *my* shorts soaking wet, or even, why is the dog covered with sand and seaweed that is now all over my backseat? Regan wasn't interested then and would not appreciate me knocking on her door now.

Next in the on-deck circle: Mom. She'd ask a million questions I didn't want to answer. She'd take me to the police, but what did I really have to offer? I could now tell them for sure who else was in the car with JJ. But I had no real proof, just the word of an at-risk kid with two strikes against him already. I still didn't know who had the gun.

Still, the police *would* listen to me. My dad's buddies

would investigate. They'd drag JJ in, subject him to serious grilling, maybe wrench the rest of the story out of him.

It was a plan, but it didn't make me feel good.

JJ pretty much said that they had threatened him. If JJ told, the gang would make him pay. I'd be responsible for that.

I laced my hands behind my head and stared at the ceiling, watching the blades of the overhead fan go round and round until they blurred together. Maybe there was another way. What would Dad have done?

My dad lived his beliefs. Family first, serving and protecting the community, baseball, and above all, I guess, justice. Sometimes it meant making sure the bad guys got put away. Other times it meant giving deserving people a hand up, a second chance. Probably hundreds of kids in trouble cycled through the precinct. He only worked with those he believed had potential, who truly wanted to improve themselves, get on the right track. And JJ Pico, whatever I felt about him, had been one of those kids.

I rolled over onto my stomach, rested my head on my arms. The obvious answer was for JJ himself to man up. It was his responsibility to go to the police and tell them who shot my dad. Whatever the cost.

The police could find a way to protect him, I

reasoned. Put him in Witness Protection or something. Maybe that would be a good thing, a chance at a fresh start for him and his family. Maybe they could take Otis. My vision of a new life for JJ was oddly comforting. If the whole truth could come out, that would be justice for my dad.

Without thinking it through, I grabbed my cell phone and scrolled to the Canine Connections contact list LuLu had provided. I sent JJ a text. **Do the right thing. You know what I mean.**

I stared at the screen even though I knew JJ wasn't about to text back. He was probably asleep, believing his conscience clear. Rex, curled up at my feet, lazily rolled over onto his back and assumed a favorite position: front paws up and bent in begging position, eyes closed, head lolled to one side, tongue hanging out.

He looked so innocent, so vulnerable. Affectionately, I stretched my foot out and ran my toes over his exposed belly, the only soft part of the pup's prickly pelt.

Rex. Still a mystery.

"What are you?" I whispered. This time I got a honking snore for an answer.

Did my dad snore? I caught myself wondering. Did my mom tease him about it? Why did it matter?

Because snoring would not be the only parallel between a mangy mutt who'd begged to be adopted and the parent who'd meant everything to me. The parent who'd never again smile that smile and tell me to "Say good night, Gracie."

The outsize digitized numbers on the alarm clock read 2:17 a.m. I was too wired to sleep. I couldn't even think straight. I pictured my brain splintering into a million little shards shooting like asteroids into the ether. Maybe that's why I allowed the *most* insane thoughts loose.

Dad was a detective. Rex often acted like one. He'd shown me Sheena in the act of stealing. He was the one who overheard Lissa's plans to break into a house. And yeah, it turned out that Jasmine had, in fact, been cheating. Just like Rex said.

Then there was JJ Pico.

Dad had placed him in Canine Connections. Separately, he'd told Regan about the organization, suggesting she train a service dog. I don't think he'd have been surprised that Regan got me to do it for her.

Which put me on a collision course with JJ Pico.

For extra insurance that JJ and I would continue to cross paths, the dog led me straight to his door.

I don't believe in reincarnation. I don't believe in being able to channel a dead person's spirit. I think psychics, tarot card "interpreters," palm readers, or anyone who claims they can contact the dead are a total scam.

Magical thinking. It was something my mom had told me from her bereavement book *The Year of Magical*

Thinking, about a woman coping with the sudden death of her husband. Magical thinking was something people, not necessarily nutcases, sometimes ended up doing when they lost someone. This woman—not crazy—refused to throw away her dead husband's shoes because a part of her, for a short period of time, thought maybe he'd come back.

I rolled out of bed and Googled "magical thinking." An instant-info overload of articles, references, medical and scientific definitions came up, most of it way over my head.

This much made sense: Magical thinking refers to irrational beliefs. When people believe they have the power to cast spells, or bestow luck or curses on others, that's one kind of magical thinking. Another kind is way more common and recognizable. Like if you sit in a certain seat in class, you'll do better. If you don't stare at the phone, it'll ring. If you turn your baseball cap backward, you'll affect the outcome of the game. Everyday stuff like that is considered magical thinking, too.

There was an article describing the magical thinking my mom's book was about. It said some people in mourning believe things can continue the way they were, and the loved one is still there in some form. Maybe *that* explained my hearing Rex talk, the conversations I *knew* I had with him.

Maybe I was a magical thinker, not a mental girl.

I peered at my snoozing pooch. He looked laughable, ridiculous, with his paws bent in the air, tongue still hanging out, drooling and snoring.

Do I really think this is Dad, come back to me in the form of a mangy mutt?

Does that count as magical thinking or just plain insanity?

The rest of the article said magical thinking was a coping mechanism, that it was okay, it didn't mean you'd gone over the edge—as long as it didn't last for such a long time that you never moved forward. Which is exactly what Regan accused me of, and my mom worried about. Me being stuck in mourning, not moving on.

I pictured the beach tonight. How when I saw the moonlight reflected on the ocean, instantly I'd thought about Dad. It was like I could feel what he felt, hear him saying, "There's just something mystical about that sight, Gracie." It didn't hurt to feel that way. It was kind of okay. Was that moving forward? Was that what Rex had been sent to do? Sent by whom?

Was Rex here to let me know that Dad was not really gone?

A strange sense of calm settled over me, feathery light and safe as a mother's, or father's, hug.

19

Life Unleashed

I woke up a few hours later no more certain about Rex, but definitely on a mission. My personal campaign to force JJ Pico to confess was on. Between classes, I barraged him with texts and voice messages. **Confession is good for the soul**. And **Tell the cops**. And **The police can protect you. Ask me how**. I wasn't surprised that he never responded. Later, at Canine Connections, I planned to harangue him in person.

Only—not so fast.

The first clue that something was different today at Canine Connections was olfactory: The place smelled great! Instead of its usual dog aroma, the scent of freshly baked sweets filled the air. I traced it to LuLu's desk, where sure enough, a platter of chocolate-chip cookies and cupcakes sat enticingly.

Rex and I tandem-salivated.

We had visitors! Their excited chatter reverberated around the room. All were kids, some with parents, some without. All disabled.

Last clue: LuLu brought the cheese. "Good *arf*-ternoon!" she joked, sounding seriously un-LuLu-like. We trooped in, Maria with Daffodil, Megan with Romeo, Lissa with Chainsaw, Trey with Clark Kent, JJ with Otis, me with Rex, all of us present—and bewildered. Were we supposed to greet the newcomers? Ignore them? Introduce ourselves? We looked to our leader for guidance.

"Take your seats, trainers," LuLu said. "As you can see, some very special guests have joined us."

"And brought cake!" Rex raved, drooling copiously.

"These people have traveled from all over the country to be here. Each one has been selected from a huge pool of applicants to receive a service dog. These are the kids that *you* have been working for, the young people your dogs will go home with!" Lulu said gleefully.

I must have gasped, since she was quick to add, "Not today, of course. There's the Public Access Test to take, and the personal pairings to be done. But the group"— she indicated the visitors—"was anxious to meet you and get a look at their new partners."

I squirmed. Of course Rex wasn't going anywhere with anyone. We did this only so Regan could rock her essay and get into college.

"For the next week or so," LuLu went on, "our guests will live in our specially equipped dorms and go through orientation. This is so we—myself and the staff at Canine Connections—can get to know each person, and better understand his or her individual needs. That way, we can decide which dog fits best with each candidate. Then we'll custom-train the dogs and their new owners together. Does that make sense?"

Not as it applied to Rex it didn't.

LuLu asked for one of the moms, a chunky round-faced lady, to address us. It was more like she beamed at us. "Hi, everyone, I'm Ronnie Souther, Kaitlyn's mom." She gestured to a little girl in a wheelchair. "On behalf of everyone, I thank you for training these wonderful animals. We're so grateful and can't wait to meet our new helpers. If you'll indulge us, each of the kids has prepared something to say to you. But there's one thing I want to say before we start, and I hope it stays with you: 'Some angels have wings, others have tails.' You guys, the trainers, are giving us our angels."

Today's weather? Sappy. With a real chance of tears.

Mrs. Souther's daughter, Kaitlyn, a spunky little girl in a wheelchair, went first. She told us she lived in Spokane, Washington, and was in third grade. Confidently, she read from her notebook. "I was born with spina bifida, which means my legs aren't too strong. I want to use crutches instead of a wheelchair in school, and with the help of a dog, I can do that and stay balanced. My dog can also help carry my school things."

I flashed on our dogs at CVS, carrying our purchases.

Kaitlyn took a breath, and scanned her paper. "Other things I want my dog to do are open the refrigerator, and . . ." A blush crept up her small neck. She turned to look at her mom, who jumped right in. "Kaitlyn has trouble getting in and out of the bathtub." She knelt to whisper in her daughter's ear. A wide grin appeared on the girl's face. "I almost forgot. I play sled hockey and my dog can help me at the tournament!"

"Sled hockey," LuLu explained, "is hockey on sleds instead of on skates. Kaitlyn also swims, plays basketball, and skis. She won first place in the butterfly stroke in the Special Olympics."

The kid was an athlete. *Cool.*

Kaitlyn wrapped up with, "I want to thank you and can't wait to meet my dog!"

Daffodil, I caught myself thinking. *The yellow Lab would be perfect for her.*

Next up was ten-year-old Hailey, who'd traveled from Kansas City. She suffered from arthrogryposis—a disability I'd never heard of. As Hailey explained, it meant her muscles were very weak and some of her joints were shorter than they should be. Even with the use of crutches, she was severely limited physically—walking, bending, and getting up were hardest. "My new dog will help me by picking up things I've dropped," she read. "He or she will be something sturdy for me to hang on to if I'm slipping. That would make me feel safe. I also want my dog to help me chase boys at recess!" Her hand flew to her mouth as an explosion of giggles erupted.

It was catching. Soon the whole room was laughing with her.

If she ends up with Romeo, I caught myself picturing it, *the boys will be running to her. With that beautiful chocolate Lab by her side, this little girl will be the center of attention— not for her disability, either.*

The stories continued, equal parts heartfelt and hopeful.

Joss, from Tennessee, lost his sight in an accident. He just got accepted to a college halfway across the country. "Going away from home for the first time will force me into a new environment," he explained. "I'll have to learn the layout of the campus, of my classes, my dorm. With a dog, it's my best chance."

Chainsaw, I immediately thought. The German shepherd had been a quick study when the dogs were learning to cross streets, avoid obstacles, and open doors. Chainsaw would be a good match for Joss.

Another boy, about my age, from Bangor, Maine, had

severe respiratory disorder. "I get very depressed," he admitted. "And I keep losing my inhaler. I heard dogs could be trained to sniff out the inhaler and bring it to me."

"Look," "find," "retrieve," "give it to me." All were basic commands the dogs had mastered. Otis. The pooch with the fewest class hours was probably the smartest. Otis could be taught what an inhaler was—he'd quickly memorize its unique odor—and learn to associate the word with the item. Bonus, the sight of that poufy poodle in his protective booties could lift the depression from a gloomy gray cloud cluster.

Thinking about Otis reminded me—time to nudge JJ. We hadn't said a word to each other since getting here, nor even made eye contact. I had a note prepared, *How can you live with yourself?*, which I folded and passed to him. I watched with dismay as he crumpled it up. Whatever. He couldn't ignore me forever.

The smallest child in the room was Daniel, only six. He didn't say anything because he couldn't. "Daniel is severely autistic," his mom explained. "He has no language, no friends, and a terrifying habit of running away. Once, he opened up a side window and crawled out of the house. It took us an hour to find him." She swallowed at the memory. "I plan to use a double leash on our new dog. When we go out, I'll hold one, and one will be attached to a harness around Daniel. That way, Daniel will stay safe." Her hopes included teaching Daniel to talk. "Seeing the dog respond to words may help our boy put words and actions together. And when he has meltdowns, I'm hoping a dog will comfort him and . . ." She had trouble finishing. "Be his friend." She dabbed her eyes. So did Maria, Megan, and even Trey.

A big dog wouldn't work for a boy so small. Clark Kent would.

Last to talk was a girl named Kim, from Orlando, Florida. She'd seemed unable to stay still throughout the class. She was all jerks and twitches and tics, her body twisted at weird angles. Haltingly, and with a speech impediment, she told us she had cerebral palsy. Her disorder isolated her from the kids at school. She saw a service dog as an icebreaker. "People are scared or intimidated because of my disability. And," she continued with difficulty, "I want to have someone who will love me no matter what I look like."

My heart clutched. I knew which dog would serve her best. But no way was I giving up Rex. I pulled him closer to me and stroked his head.

"Is it time for cookies?" he asked, looking up at me hopefully.

I'll give you all the cookies you want—if you just stay.

∾

I hadn't said anything about today's Canine Connections class, but at dinner I sulked in silence, pushing the food around the plate.

My mom thought she knew why. "Tomorrow is going to be a tough one," she acknowledged, reaching out to cover my hand with hers.

"Tomorrow?" I repeated numbly.

"June second. Dad's birthday," Regan reminded me. "*You*, of all people, forgot?"

I was horrified. Forgetting the first birthday my dad didn't live to see felt like a betrayal. "Can I be excused?" I mumbled, anxious to get away.

"No, you cannot," Regan responded sternly.

"What?" Who was she to boss me around? She'd had a *party* when she should have been grieving.

Even Mom looked at her with surprise. "Of course Grace can go if she wants."

"Ugh." Regan rolled her eyes and pushed herself away from the table. "I was going to wait until after dinner. But since little miss pouty puss is about to lock herself away, I'll do it now." With that, my big sister dramatically strode off. She returned a minute later bearing gifts.

"What is this?" Mom asked. Regan had given us identically wrapped presents. Judging by the gifts' shape and heft, I would have guessed a large-sized book, but I couldn't picture my sister making it past the café in Barnes & Noble.

"Open it," she said. "It's to celebrate tomorrow."

Celebrate? Without him? Even in Regan's "getting back to normal" world, that was so wrong.

Mom went first. I watched her expression change from perplexed to touched as she extracted a large framed photograph, and lovingly ran her finger across it. I leaned over to see. It was a candid of Mom and Dad strolling on the beach, holding hands, eyes on each other. It was a fairly recent shot, and among the most beautiful I'd ever seen of them.

"I remember when you took this picture, Regan." Mom's voice was thick with emotion. "Where'd you find it?"

"In the trash heap that Grace calls her room," she answered. "When *I* was cleaning it up."

"Go on, Grace," Mom urged. "Open yours."

The photo took my breath away. It was a close-up of Dad and me. I must have been around eight. My arms were draped around his neck, my head rested on his shoulder, my hair tickled his shoulder blades. I wasn't smiling, but the look in my eyes said it all: I had absolute faith that this man, my daddy, would protect me and love me unconditionally. Forever.

My throat was closed to traffic—due to the lump that suddenly formed and blocked the passageway.

"Anyway, she has a ton of pictures in there," Regan blithely babbled, "completely disorganized."

"They were just snapshots," I managed to croak out while staring at my younger face. "Blown up they look so . . . amazing."

The one she'd chosen for herself surprised me. It didn't center on Regan, but was a photo from when we were a family of four.

"There were so many to choose from," Regan said softly, almost like she was talking to herself, "but these, they spoke to me, if you know what I mean." A lone teardrop spilled from Regan's exquisite eye.

20

Testing Rex

I should have been dreading the Public Access Test. Except that would mean I'd actually thought about it.

Unfortunately, no matter what I thought, or didn't think, it *was* coming. Soon. Like final exams, heat waves, and hurricane season. Even though I'd chosen to ignore its existence, I knew exactly what it was. And what it meant.

The Public Access Test was the moment of truth for our dogs, and by extension, us. Had we trained them well enough? Were they confident? Did they respond correctly to commands? Were they able to ignore distractions and laser-focus on their owner? Could we really trust Romeo, Daffodil, Chainsaw, Otis, and Clark Kent to keep a disabled kid safe?

I knew Rex could.

And, in other circumstances, I'd have proudly handed him over with confidence. He'd be a life-changer for a physically challenged kid.

Now? Giving him up was unthinkable. Rex had come home with us for a reason, which I was only just starting to grasp.

I rationalized everything else away. Regan's essay could still be written as planned. We had, after all, rescued a pound dog and totally trained him to be a service dog. The college wouldn't care what happened next. Bet they wouldn't even check up. Rex's future would not impact Regan's.

As for Kim, the girl with cerebral palsy who'd probably benefit most from Rex? I felt a little guilty about that, but she'd totally get another highly trained dog. If there isn't one available from Canine Connections, she could get one from any of the other amazing assistance dog training programs. She didn't specifically need *Rex*.

I did.

But how to keep him with me? It all hinged on that test. If he passed, he'd be gone. It was like a missile: once launched, there was no calling it back. He'd go directly from a passing grade to a new home. I saw only one option here.

Rex had to fail.

There are three reasons a trained service dog might get disqualified. He's either too fearful, too easily startled, or too aggressive and can't be trusted. Rex had none of those issues, and left to his own devices, he'd ace the test. It was up to me to make sure that didn't happen.

I went with bribery.

I described in delicious detail the entire turkey carcass entrée and steak bones side dish I would prepare for him—if he did exactly what I said. I spent every moment alone with him for the next three days, drilling this in. Rex was to deliberately disobey LuLu or whoever administered his test. He was to sit when told "Forward." He would not stop at curbs. He'd bring the remote control when specifically asked for the leash. I showed him how to look confused when given the command to push the elevator button, flip the light switch, or tug the door handle. Rex had to get his dunce dog on, while using his smarts to concentrate on *my* instructions and no one else's. He had to remember only one thing—the sumptuous, savory feast that awaited.

Rex was on board. Or so he droolingly assured me every time I mentioned that turkey carcass.

Still, when the day of the test arrived, I felt only semisecure delivering him to Canine Connections. The whole class was there. We trainers anxiously hovered outside the testing room, chatting and reassuring one another that his or her dog would pass. I felt sure I was the only one hoping my dog got an F.

As it turned out, I had the shortest wait. Although they'd all gone in together, Rex was the first dog to finish the test. It reminded me of a jury returning a verdict quickly, which according to TV shows, means everyone was in instant agreement. The defendant was clearly innocent. Or obviously guilty.

Whatever Rex had done—innocently obeyed me or guiltily performed for the instructors—he'd done it wholeheartedly. He gave me no clue, verbal or otherwise, no matter how much I pestered him. I decided to be positive and assume the best. I gave him his reward.

∾

Bad move. The dog didn't deserve it. If he hadn't already digested the turkey when LuLu called later that night with the test results, I would have demanded it back. LuLu didn't even have to say it; she had me at "Hi, Grace!"

Rex had passed the Public Access Test "with flying colors," she crowed. I sank down on my bed. She was so proud of both of us, Rex and me. She glowingly recited the play-by-play action, reviewing how brilliantly my dog had performed. She was so elated, she didn't seem to notice I'd gone mute.

After a few minutes, LuLu's tone switched from thrilled to thoughtful. Did I have any feelings about which candidate to pair him with? What did I think about the child with spina bifida, or perhaps the blind college student? Or maybe Kim, the last girl who'd spoken?

I couldn't answer. I was fast-forwarding through the stages of grief.

1. Denial—Surely, LuLu had accidentally called the wrong person. 'Cause Rex had promised to *fail* the test.
2. Anger—How could Rex betray me? We had an agreement, a pact, a *bond*. How could he break it?
3. Bargaining—Was there some reason I could come up with to prove Rex had cheated on the test? Could I say I gave him doggy 'roids or something else that might invalidate his score? Or what if I, oops, just found out that he'd never had his shots?
4. Depression—Sadness seeped in as I flipped the phone shut. What if this was really happening?
5. Acceptance is the last stage of grief. I was nowhere near ready for that.

I found it odd that the star of this debacle was not at his usual post, cozied up at the foot of my bed. Nor was he sniffing for a random crumb under some pile in my room. Rex-the-betrayer was nowhere in sight.

Coincidence? I think not. Dogs, like people, know when they have something to feel guilty about. I stalked down the hallway, calling his name.

It was my mom who answered. "He's with me, Grace. We're watching TV in the living room."

I came upon such a sweet scene, I almost went into sugar shock. Rex was curled up on the couch, his head resting on my mom's lap. She was tenderly stroking his spiky coat. Both pairs of eyes, human and canine, were glued to the TV.

"We're watching this unbelievable show on cable called *My Dog Ate WHAT?*" Mom supplied the answer to a question I hadn't asked. "Come sit with us."

"I don't think so," I said, grabbing Rex by the collar, yanking him off the couch.

"Hey, I was watching that!" Rex groused, trying to wriggle away from me.

Mom was taken aback. "He's barking because you're being so rough with him. What'd he do?"

"He knows exactly what he did," I said through gritted teeth, tightening my grip on his collar. "Let's go, Rex."

Tail tucked between his legs, the hapless hound

grudgingly complied. I'd barely shut the door to my room before lacing into him. "How could you do that?"

"Do what?" he asked, all innocence and ignorance, one ear pointed up, the other flopped over.

"How could you pass the Public Access Test? We had a deal!"

"Which test was that?" Rex used the exact expression of confusion I'd taught him only yesterday.

I pinned him with a demonic stare. "The one you took this morning. I specifically told you *not* to follow commands. Why did you disobey me?"

I swear Rex shrugged his shoulder blades. "I have a natural instinct to want to please. And it was for LuLu. I like her so much!" His tail started to wag, but thought better of it.

"Did she have a treat in her hand during the test?" I asked suspiciously.

"They were on the desk behind her. I knew I'd get one," he confessed.

"Rex, we had a deal! I told you about the turkey carcass! Instead you sold me out for a Snausage?"

"It was a Yummy Chummy Bacon Bit, but that's not the point. Dogs live in the moment, Stacey. We don't think about something that's coming later."

"But, Rex, you're not a dog. I mean, you're not *just* a dog."

"I'm not?" There was that confused look again, tilting his snout to the side, pendulum-like.

I was exasperated. I knelt to his level and cradled his head in my hands, forcing him to look at me. "Don't you get it? They're going to send you to live with someone else."

Rex wiggled away from me. "Don't be silly, Tracey! This is you and me! We'll always be together."

No, we won't. Not unless I can figure some way out of this mess.

I spent the rest of the night racking my brain to think of a way to keep Rex. 'Cause no matter where he was "supposed" to go, or whom he was slated to be paired with . . . well, he just wasn't. No way was Rex abandoning me. Not him, too. Only . . . nothing I could think of was even halfway plausible—not enough to get Rex's "flying colors" scores knocked down, or disqualify him altogether. There was no way to guarantee his continued presence in my life, to make sure he didn't leave.

Except the one I kept coming back to. It meant relying on Regan. An oxymoron if ever there was one.

∾

My sister was in the car, about to back out of our driveway, when I swung into the passenger seat. "Mom said you're going to Whole Foods. I'll come with."

"Suit yourself, Armani." Regan, in high spirits, peeled down the street.

"Listen," I said, buckling myself in, "I need to talk to you."

"Articulate."

"Where'd you get that word from?" I asked, momentarily distracted.

"I got it off a tweet. And I'm sure I heard you use it."

"Perfect segue," I said.

"Segway? The scooter?" Her smooth brow wrinkled a tad.

I closed my eyes. I'd better be prepared to help her a *lot* in senior year—a sterling college application was one thing, her grades would also be taken into account. I drew a breath and patiently explained. "I need a favor from you."

She waved dismissively. "Obviousity."

"Huh?"

"A new word. I made it up." It takes so little for Regan to be proud of herself.

"It's a pretty big favor," I warned her. "This is me, being selfish."

Her laughter unnerved me. "You don't have a selfish bone in your body."

"Yeah, I do. Although," I quickly amended, "this is for all of us. Our family."

Then I told her about Rex.

Not the talking part.

And not about how I think he might be, in some bizarre way that defies explanation or sense, channeling the spirit of our dad . . . if not his actual reincarnation.

I simply told Regan that we needed to pull Rex out of the Canine Connections program. That she just had to trust me. He could not leave us.

Then I sat ramrod straight, hands in my lap, ready to counter any argument she could come up with. I'd thought them all through and had my rebuttals ready. In my mind, our conversation went like this:

Regan: But what about my essay? He has to help a disabled person.

Me: Your essay will rock. Trust me. Plus, they'll never check up.

Regan: What if they do?

Me: Work with me, Regan.

Regan: I don't understand—remind me—why aren't we letting Rex do what you trained him to do?

Me: We *are*—eventually. I'm not ready to let him go. He's helping me, just like you said. I'm going out more—

This entire dialogue was running in my head like a scroll at the bottom of a screen, so Regan had to repeat herself before I heard what she actually said.

"Sure. No problem."

"No problem?" I repeated, dumbly.

"Grace, *you* talked *me* into adopting him. *You* trained him. If you want to put the brakes on"—for emphasis, she tapped the brake—"if you don't want him in the program, he's out. Simple."

Had my head hit the windshield? Did I suffer a concussion? Regan was putting *my* needs before her own? Who was this sweet, generous soul at the wheel and what had she done with my it's-all-about-me sister?

As if in answer, Regan smashed her foot down on the gas pedal and we vaulted forward, weaving in and out of traffic. "Like I said, Grace, you did all the work—it's your decision. I'll not only support you, I'll handle Mom, too."

"For real?" I was totally suspect.

"For reals."

"What do I have to do in return? What's the favor you need?"

Her bare bronzed shoulders contracted and relaxed. "Nothing."

It made no sense. Unless . . . Regan, too, in some spiritual, soul-deep way, knew about Rex, who he really was, or might be? Was that even possible? At this point, I was willing to believe anything.

I should have felt triumphant. Instead, I trailed Regan through the wide colorful aisles of Whole Foods awash in confusion, splashed with fear and guilt. What was *that* about?

·· 21 ··

Say Good Night, Gracie

Grace, can you get the door?" Regan called from her room. She was taking pictures of herself in different outfits and texting them to her friends. Even without Sheena, Regan's bench of besties was deep. I pictured frantic fingers flying across tiny keyboards, rushing to tell Regan how cool she looked. I wondered how many times the word "amazing" had been used.

Me, I was in my room doing actual homework, draped in a long, *amazingly* not-cute Jupiter Hammerheads T-shirt. Its logo was supposed to be a hammerhead shark, but instead it resembled some sort of red-and-black-beaked bird not found in nature.

The doorbell rang a second time.

"Grace!" Regan yelled again.

"On it," I called back as I hauled myself off the bed.

It was Monday night, only a day after Regan had agreed to let me pull Rex from the program. I had to be nice to her. A quick glance at the clock confirmed that it was after ten p.m. My mom was out to dinner and a movie with her support group—for a panicked second, I pictured a policeman at the door with bad news. My stomach twisted. It actually relaxed when I saw JJ Pico's physique illuminated under the porch light.

Was he here to tell me in person to stop harassing him with texts? Had he brought backup? I glanced over his shoulder for any sign of a car, but saw only JJ's rusty bike sprawled sideways across the driveway.

JJ himself seemed a bit disoriented. His foot was doing a nervous tap dance, his forehead beaded with sweat, yet he was rubbing his palms together as if he were chilled. If I didn't know better, I'd think he was some terrorized kid instead of a gang trainee. I wasn't inviting him in.

My "what are you doing here?" and his "I have to tell you something" overlapped, canceling each other out. Rex took that moment to brush past me and plant his bristly backside atop JJ's sneakered feet. As if the boy was giving off a needy vibe.

"I know it's late, but I need to say this." JJ's eyes were downcast.

"Articulate." I cannot believe I just mimicked Regan.

"I went to the cops, to the police station . . ." He hesitated, as if trying to decide how to proceed.

"They brought you in for questioning?" Instantly, I was alert, anticipatory.

JJ shook his head. "I went on my own."

My heart clutched. Was it possible? Had he—?

"I told them," he confirmed. "I told the cops."

Blood rushed to my ears, pounding loudly. *Easy,* I told myself. *This might not mean he confessed everything.* I stepped outside and quietly closed the door behind me.

JJ planted himself on the porch ledge. I remained standing. "What did you tell them?"

"I gave up Hector." JJ paused, then swallowed. "He had the gun. He was the one who shot Detective Abernathy."

"And the others?" I asked, my heart racing wildly now.

He nodded. "Yeah, Chris and Tony. And maybe Chris was trying to stop Hector, at the last minute, like, to swipe the gun away."

I frowned, less inclined to give the brute credit for good intentions.

"So anyway," JJ continued. "They asked me stuff. Like, was it a drive-by? Why so close to the precinct? Didn't we know we'd get caught?"

"What did you say?"

"Like I told you, I wasn't in on the planning. Even

now, I still don't know if Hector meant to shoot the tires, like he said. Or . . ." He trailed off with a shrug.

"Why *did* they do it so close to the police station?"

"Maybe they were just showing off for me, like, look what we can get away with, right on the cop's turf. 'Cause if they could chase Detective A away from me, that was the point."

I blinked. A dumbass gang of teens thought they could intimidate my dad? My eyes fell on Rex, who gave me such a sad look, I nearly lost it. Dogs, all of them, have compassion.

"So anyway, I figured you'd want to know," JJ said.

"Are you scared?" That came out before I could stop it—why should I care?

"Every freakin' second," JJ admitted ruefully, "but that's nothing new."

I scrunched my forehead, unsure what he meant.

"They never trusted me, Hector or any of them. If I was listening to Detective A, then I wasn't one of them. And if I wasn't with them, Hector used to say, 'Big mistake, man. Your bro would not be happy.'"

"But you stayed in my dad's program anyway," I said, just starting to see how hard it must've been for him. The gang had a strong pull—in a twisted way, they were like his family. Then my dad came along, seeing something worth saving in JJ. Maybe JJ telling the truth, finally, was the proof that Dad had been right.

"Thanks," I said shakily.

"You're the one who really pushed me to do it."

"With all those texts?"

"Nah. Those were stupid." He waved me away. "It's what you said. It stayed with me."

"All the work he put into you will have been for nothing?" I guessed.

"You said that if I was really grateful to him, I should honor him. I should do what he always told me. If I knew something was the right thing to do, I should be brave and do it even if I was scared—"

"Especially if you're scared," I finished for him, my voice anything but triumphant. JJ had made his choice. I still had one of my own to make, and it scared me to death.

I watched JJ ride away, staring as the reflecting light on the bike seat got smaller and smaller, until it was just a pinprick, and the night swallowed him.

It's over. Nothing can bring my dad back, but Detective Gregory Abernathy will finally get the justice he deserves. And I played a big role in that. So why wasn't I dancing on the ceiling, jumping for joy?

And what would happen to JJ now? Did doing the right thing make him a target for the thugs?

Or would he eventually end up back with the gang anyway? Is it possible that he would stay strong and continue on the path my dad started him on?

I turned it over in my mind. There was only one conclusion I could come to. My dad believed in JJ. That's enough for me.

I should call my mom. I should race to Regan's room. But all at once, I felt so very, very tired. All I wanted to do was sleep.

It wasn't until I'd reached my room that I realized Rex hadn't followed me. I called his name, but got no response. Had I accidentally locked him out? I retraced my steps and opened the door. No dog. "Rex! Where are you?" I called. "It's time for bed."

No answer. I checked the kitchen, but the chowhound wasn't there. Nor was he in the living room, bathroom, or any of the bedrooms. I finally found a pooped-looking pooch the last place I looked, belly-down in the tiny mudroom.

"Come, we're going to bed," I said.

"I think I'll hang out here. It's cooler." His tail brushed the floor.

"I'll open the window in my room and turn the overhead fan on," I offered.

"That's okay, Francie."

Not okay. Rex hadn't spent a night in any room but mine since he got here. Was he upset about something? He'd heard JJ's confession. Maybe the dog . . . who certainly was not just a dog . . . needed his space?

"Do you want to talk about it?" I knelt and scratched behind his ears.

"I'm good," he assured me, closing his eyes.

"You know you can stay with us, right? I already told you we're pulling you out of Canine Connections. You don't have to go live with someone else."

Rex flicked his eyes open but didn't say anything.

"Are you sick?" I asked.

His head jerked up. "Sick? No way! I feel great! The tiles here are so nice and cool on my belly. Besides, it's closer to the kitchen."

I gave up and started down the hallway. "If you change your mind, you know how to tug open the door to my room."

"Wait," Rex called.

I spun on my heel. "What is it, Rex?" The dog was looking at me with big, soulful eyes.

"Aren't you going to say good night, Gracie?"

I stopped breathing.

Say good night, Gracie.

The dog had called me every name except my own—and *now* he comes out with it? Only my dad called me Gracie. I thought I'd never hear those words again.

I began to take short, rapid breaths. I felt my chin tremble, and though I bit my lip, it quavered, too. Acid tinged my throat, my eyes watered, stinging. I could feel my entire body welling up like a balloon being filled with air—only it kept going, bigger, bigger, and bigger, and I couldn't stop the explosion. I did not cry prettily like Regan, or weep discreetly like Mom. I burst into a sobbing, snot-dripping, hiccupping mess. My whole body shook so badly, I dropped to my knees, wrapped myself around the pound dog, and wept loudly enough to wake the dead.

·· 22 ··

Say Anything

Mom stumbled upon me in the morning, curled up in a ball next to the dog. Her gasp woke me. "Grace—have you been here all night? Were you crying?"

"I . . . guess so," I said groggily. I knew my eyes were puffy, my cheeks stained with tears and dried mucus.

Reaching down to help me up, she asked nervously, "Did something happen?"

Only everything.

A little later, over a crunchy bowl of oatmeal, I carefully downloaded Mom on JJ's confession—leaving out the part about meeting him at the beach at night. My mom gripped and twisted a tissue throughout, but never once stopped to question me or voice any doubts. She hugged me hard. "I'm so proud of you, Grace." Her voice was thick with emotion. "My baby—this has been hardest on you. And here you are, the one who brings us closure." Then she shook her head. "I can't believe I just said that. I hate that word."

Me too.

Mom probably heard it a lot in her support group. I heard it all the time, from nearly everyone—teachers, other adults, even kids my age.

"What does that even mean?" I said. I pictured it like a race. Once you cross the finish line, you're done. It's over. It's officially time to stop mourning and move on. My personal finish line is like the horizon—you can swim the whole entire ocean and never get there.

My mom said, "Well, it means that finding out what really happened to your father helps in the healing process."

"I don't want to heal. It would be like our lives with him never happened."

"That's not it, Grace. The idea is that with time—with each passing day—it's supposed to hurt a little less. The pain will always be there. That doesn't ever go away completely. But eventually, it will feel okay to go on with your life, to smile, laugh—dance."

"Didn't take Regan too long," I said. But I could no longer drum up any righteous anger at my sister. She didn't grieve for Dad the way I did, and I was not okay with that. Her coping methods were different, but I was beginning to wonder if that made them less worthy of respect.

"You knew your father maybe better than anyone in this family," my mom interrupted my thoughts. "Do you really think he would have wanted you to be sad forever?"

I pictured my dad's big grin, his twinkling eyes, his off-the-wall sense of humor, love of music, and inept dancing. His bear hugs.

It was my turn to hug my mother.

∾

Hours later, I decided to play catch with Rex in the backyard. The dog had been acting . . . I don't know, a little droopy or something ever since we got up this morning. He'd been unusually quiet, too. An invigorating game of "get it," "bring it" was sure to cheer him up.

Now that we were playing, however, it became clear the dog didn't actually need cheering up. Rex acted his usual hyper-excited self, racing after the balls I tossed. His tail, that hairy propeller, was in overdrive. He launched himself into the air to intercept each ball before it hit the ground. Dutifully, he dropped each one at my feet, panting fiercely, waiting for me to toss another. He barked, he yipped, he even whined once.

But he didn't say anything.

Which was odd for the chatterbox.

I tried to tease a few words out of him. "What's the matter, cat got your tongue?"

Rex tilted his head to one side, then the other. Like he didn't understand.

Neither did I. What, had Rex gotten shy all of a sudden?

"Are you having fun?" I asked.

"Woof, woof!" was all I got in return.

"Are you thirsty? Do you want some water?" I tried.

In response, he leaped and tried to grab the ball out of my hand. "Okay, okay, I'll throw it," I said.

Bright-eyed, Rex panted his approval.

I didn't know what else to do—or say—so I just lobbed the ball again.

My cell phone, tucked in my pocket, signaled an incoming text.

"Hang on," I said to Rex while I checked it out.

Movies & Cheesecake Factory in 1 hr, Mercy had written. I hesitated. Then I texted her back.

∾

The movie, a cheesy rom-com, was mindless and the popcorn supersize, just the way I liked it. Between the four of us—Jasmine, Kendra, Mercy, and me—we devoured it.

We shouldn't have been hungry for dinner, but the Cheesecake Factory beckoned, and miraculously there was no wait. We slid into a booth.

"What I love most about this place," Mercy said, flipping through the spiral-bound menu, "is that my mother hates it."

"Go for it," said Kendra. "Order something really decadent."

"That's my plan—something deep-fried and over-salted with zero nutritional value," Mercy quipped. "Or, you know what? A Green Chile Cheeseburger could also satisfy."

I looked at the ingredients: spicy green chiles, melted cheese, and onions with tortilla strips, salsa, and chipotle mayo.

Mercy wasn't done. "French fries on the side. And for dessert, Reese's peanut butter chocolate cake cheesecake."

"I'll have what she's having." I pointed to Mercy when the waiter came to take the order.

Kendra went for pasta and an extra fork to dip into Mercy's dessert. Only Jasmine stuck with a salad. "The dance is next week. I will fit in that dress," she said defensively.

"Right, like one meal is going to make a difference," Mercy scoffed.

"Speaking of the dance." Kendra caught my eye. "Maybe you'll change your mind? Now that things are more"—she paused, looking down as she settled the napkin on her lap—"resolved?"

She meant JJ's confession. I'd told my friends the Twitter version of the story—very limited. I wasn't ready to confide more. And I totally wasn't ready to get dressed up and pretend to be upbeat for the eighth-grade dance. "I don't think my groove thing is up to shaking," I tried to joke. "I'm not sure if I have one."

What I didn't say: I was afraid of a music-caused meltdown. There are certain old songs always played at school dances, bar mitzvahs, weddings. Like "Livin' on a Prayer" by Bon Jovi. That was the one my dad and I—and Regan, too, now that I think about it—used to try and outsing each other to see who could punch the air higher. And for the slow dance, if they played "In Your Eyes," I'd fall apart. It was my mom and dad's wedding song. Plus, who knew what else I might be ambushed with. Hearing those songs on my iPod was one thing—bursting into tears in front of a hundred kids was something else.

Before Kendra could try to convince me, the orders arrived.

"Anyway," said Jasmine, measuring out a teaspoon of dressing to sprinkle on her salad, "I'm just glad I'm getting to go."

Right. I'd almost forgotten that part of Jasmine's punishment for cheating in French was a ban on all extra-curricular activities. Like it wasn't bad enough she got three days' suspension and an F for the semester. Luckily, they'd relented on the dance.

I suddenly lost my appetite. I'd never know if she got caught because the teacher got suspicious when my own failing grades suddenly soared, and my answers matched Jasmine's exactly. That's because I never confessed. Mercy wouldn't let me.

"*You* didn't do anything wrong," she insisted.

I hadn't *meant* to do anything wrong.

"You need the passing grade," Mercy lectured me. "Besides, unless she told you *how* she was getting the answers, you couldn't have known anything. Not for sure."

Yeah, I could.

∾

When I got home that evening, Rex overgreeted me, nearly knocking me down by jumping on me and licking my face as if he hadn't seen me in days. His eyes were bright as he raced around me so speedily that his tail actually created a breeze. When he trotted away from me it was only to return a minute later with my mitt in his jaw.

I laughed, heartened by this shower of affection. "I

guess you're feeling better! So what was bothering you before? Were you shocked into silence because of JJ?"

Rex dropped the baseball mitt at my feet, darted into the mudroom, and returned with my softball. I stroked his head. "Right, I get it. You're multitalented, you can act just like a regular dog. But we both know you're not. So . . . let's have it, Rex, say something. Say anything."

Rex titled his head as if he didn't understand. Then he barked.

·· 23 ··

The Essay!

I loooove you, I looove you, Get up! Walk me!" No, Rex didn't say that—he had not miraculously regained the ability of speech overnight, but by now I was used to the daily wake-up call, the full-frontal face licking. Even as early as—I checked the clock—five a.m.?

"No way," I said to Rex. "Unless you talk to me. Then I'll get up."

The dog's tongue was hanging out, his tail going a mile a minute, but no words were forthcoming. I scrunched down in the bed and pulled the covers over my head. Then I got a text.

Who was up at this hour? Curious, I grabbed the cell phone. Regan? She never texted me, not if we were both home. Her style of communicating is barging into my room without knocking.

Need a favor, she'd written.

Of course you do. I rolled my eyes.

Please read e-mail.

Okay, that was enough to get me out of bed. Under "subject," Regan had put **Favor**. Her message was, **Can you check this for mistakes?**

The attachment was titled Parsons School for Design, Writing Sample.

I'd almost forgotten my offer to help her, but did remember that her effort had been pretty lame, and needed a lot of work. I wasn't intending to read it right now. I opened it only to see if she'd actually attached it.

Then I read it.

Surprise number one: This was a brand-new effort. She'd deleted her first try and started all over.

Surprise number two: She'd changed her topic. Originally, she picked the one that highlighted her self-less volunteer work training a service dog. This wasn't that. This topic was "someone who's had a significant influence on you."

Whopper of a surprise: She'd chosen . . . me? How would this make her look good to the college? And if it didn't . . . again, *where* had my selfish sister gone, and who is this selfless person impersonating her?

The writing was still lame, and her run-on sentences, non sequiturs, gratuitous overuse of exclamation points, "like," and "totally" made her sound like a ditzy beauty pageant contestant. But as I read on, I realized there was something else that might outweigh her mistakes. She'd told the truth.

The person who's had a significant influence on me is my sister, Grace, and she's my younger sister! I think she would be surprised that I picked her, because probably I don't show it. In our family (besides our mom) there's only two of us and it's like these roles were given to us when we were born. I'm the social one, the total girly girl who really cares about fashion, and what I look like is very important to me. I have a lot of friends. Grace is the smart one. She always gets As and she reads a lot and likes baseball. Some people think she should try to be more like me, but I wish I could be like her!

It's not because she's smarter then me, and it's not that she's very nice. Even though she thinks I'm superficial, she always does favors for me. It's because she's brave. Being brave was not something

I thought affected me. But she showed me that it's very important.

In November, our dad died. It was sad for all of us. I didn't know what to do except continue doing what I usually do. Going to school, hanging out with my friends and designing fashions, which is my passion, and why I want to attend your school, which is the best in the world for that.

Grace stopped doing everything she used to do. She shut herself in her room and wouldn't talk to her friends. She wasn't worried that she could lose them, even though she doesn't have a lot. She hardly ate. She lost weight, which most girls would be happy about, but I don't think she cares. She stopped doing her schoolwork, and got Fs. That was maybe the worst thing because she's naturally smart and I think she's proud of her normal good grades.

The only activity she did was a favor for me. She took this dog that we adopted to school to learn to help disabled people. She did that, like, three times a week, even though I was supposed to do it. I was always too busy.

I kept telling her it was time to stop acting like a freak and get back to her normal life. She would answer that life would never be normal again because Dad's not here.

I thought she was only making things harder for herself, but now I realize that she was being really brave. My sister didn't care what other people thought of her. She didn't try to hide her real feelings and act like things were totally okay. She was not okay. And she was okay with not being okay. Does that make sense? I think it's brave to show how you really feel even if those feelings are downers. I couldn't do that. I didn't want to lose my friends or mess up my grades. I want to get into your school and that was all I thought about. I even adopted the dog because it might make me look better on my application. I know that doesn't make me look good. But in the end, because of my sister, the world has one more dog who could one day give a disabled person a new life. I didn't contribute so much when the dog was in training, but I'd like to contribute now. As you will see, the original designs I am now submitting serve an actual purpose for the service dog. As well as being fashion-forward, which you don't normally see.

Design # 1: Waterproof Burberry-inspired booties, leash, and matching cone to shield a dog's eyes in the rain.

Design # 2: Sequined reflective vests to wear at night with slim, stylish side packs.

Design #3: Denim outfits with selection of custom patches depicting peace signs, Harley-Davidson bikes, whatever the disabled person's cause is.

If the admissions people at Parsons judged Regan by the structure, grammar, or even content of her essay, I had my work cut out for me. On the other hand, if humility and killer designs counted, she was, like, so totally in!

·· 24 ··

Profoundly Regan

Night stretched into day, homework into late-night TV, sleep into wakefulness. By the minute, my stomach twisted into more knots. Several times a day, I'd ask, "Are you sick, Rex? Should we go to the vet?" Even as I asked, it was clear the dog was as healthy as he'd ever been. He hoovered his food, begged for more. He was playful, emotive, and vocal even. Just not with words.

I was completely over-the-top obsessing about Rex. It'd been days—days!—and the dog still hadn't uttered one word. He didn't respond to my entreaties or fistfuls of treats, my pouts or shouts. The irony was inescapable. A dog *not* talking made less sense to me than the other way around.

In spite of that, I was having banner days in school. I'd scraped by in math, rocked science, and met Mr.

Kassan's great expectations with my essay on *The Pig-man & Me*. The teacher was all over it, even posted it on the bulletin board with a chunky A+ stamped at the top. Best of all, the language arts teacher didn't ruin it by saying something cheesy like "Guess you were ready."

It was only at the final bell on one random Tuesday that I realized I hadn't thought about my dad all day long. It felt weird, but not betrayal-weird. Honestly, I was more concerned about Rex.

Plus, I'd yet to tell LuLu of my plans. Training was over and Canine Connections was closed until September. The staff was probably occupied now that the recipients were there for their orientation and training. I could have left a voice mail, but that felt wrong. If I was definite about pulling Rex from the program, I wanted to take the dog over there, thank her for everything.

Maybe I wanted her to say that keeping him was okay.

Time was running out. I'd have to reach her before Sunday, the big graduation ceremony when the pairings were announced. It wouldn't be fair to promise Rex to a new family.

This family needed him. I needed him to talk! I started sounding like Annie Sullivan, trying to coax a word out of Helen Keller, or my French teacher, tirelessly repeating proper pronunciation. I got down to his level and slowly said things he associated with yummy-ness, like "Snausage." Or "Pup-Peroni." Or "I love you."

Another time, I went into scolding-mommy mode.

I swore I'd withhold treats until he told me—in words—that he wanted some. Rex reacted by snatching the Scooby Snack out of my hand.

I told him he wasn't allowed on the bed until he asked properly. The disobedient dog jumped up anyway.

I threatened him with not getting up early to walk him—unless he woke me verbally. He blithely let himself out. He had been trained, after all, to open doors.

Finally, I tried to scare him into talking.

I warned him that I'd go ahead and send him off with another family unless he talked. Rex reacted by displaying his normal over-the-top good nature.

Then I got really desperate. I said I wasn't petting him anymore. And that he was banned from my room. I'd kick him out if he tried. I'd lock the door.

Not even those dire threats worked. He rolled over on his back, waiting for me to rub his tummy. It was too hard not to.

When he still hadn't uttered a word by Saturday night, I lied spectacularly, and shouted that if he didn't say anything, I might have to stop loving him. Hearing those words coming out of my mouth, and still not one from Rex, tripped a switch in me. I went on a rant, like the crazy person I used to think I was. It went something like this: "What's wrong with you? Why are you doing this to me? Are you punishing me? I can't believe you'd be so selfish! After all we did for you! I hate you!!" That last bit came with major sobbing.

And banging on the door.

"You want to dial it down, sister?" Regan demanded as she stormed in. "I'm trying to concentrate."

"On what, yourself?"

"Oooh, back to your usual sarcastic self, I see. If you must know, I'm creating a new fashion." Regan started to describe it, but I cut her off.

"You don't understand. Something's wrong with Rex!"

My sister shifted her gaze to the pooch, whose eyes shone and tail wagged happily. She grabbed the softball and tossed it onto my bed. In a microsecond, Rex leaped up and brought it back to her.

"Seems fine to me," she said. "He's acting like a dog."

"That's just the problem!" My voice was strained, loud. "He's not just a dog!"

"Well, I know that," Regan said.

"You do?" Was she about to tell me something . . . huge? Was it too much to hope that Regan understood about Rex? That's why she agreed to let him stay?

"You're not just any dog, are you, Rex?" Regan cooed. "You're not cute, but it's like the way designers see their fashions, like their babies. Other people might think they're ugly, but to the person who created them, they're beautiful."

I thought my head would explode, but my composure was first to go. I was now half screeching, half wailing—all begging. "He talks! Regan, he talks. Really. I'm not crazy. Rex has been talking to me ever since the day at the shelter. That's why I adopted him. He told me to." I collapsed onto the floor and waited for it. For Regan to tell me I'm wackadoodle, or be so horrified, to call Mom. Or 911. Or . . . simply roll her eyes and walk away.

But Regan had not moved. She stood stock-still, arms crossed, shifting her eyes from Rex to me and back again. Almost as if she was taking me seriously.

Regan lowered her whole self onto the carpet and began to gently pet Rex. Something she rarely, if ever, did. At least without complaining that he needed a shampoo, smelled funny, or should go to a doggy spa. Meanwhile, Rex responded to her touch with the sweet sounds of doggy bliss.

Finally Regan turned to me. "Remind me—what's the problem?"

"The problem," I whined, "is that he stopped. He stopped *talking*—completely. It's been, like, over a week. All he's done is bark, whimper, and make the sound he's making now."

Regan was silent.

"You don't believe me, do you?" I asked the obvious question. And before I could stop myself, I dissolved into unpretty sobs.

Regan uncoiled herself, got up, and strode over to my nightstand, where she plucked a tissue out of the box. "Here." She waved it in my face. "Blow your nose."

I obeyed.

Then Regan knelt again, this time in front of me. She tucked my hair, which had stuck onto my wet cheek, behind my ear. I looked at her, bewildered.

"Here's the thing, Grace," she said carefully. "This dog has always been . . . I don't know . . . like there's something different about him. But to say he talks? That's pretty over-the-top, even for you."

"So you don't believe me. Why should—"

She cut me off. "I do. I believe that you believe it. That he talked, I mean."

I croaked, "Why did he stop, then?"

And then Regan said something that broke and healed my heart at the same time.

"Maybe you finally heard what he had to say."

· · 25 · ·

Some Angels Have Wings, Others Have Tails

It was the last Sunday in June. I was in the Jupiter High School auditorium, sweltering one minute, chilled the next—uncomfortable in every way possible. But there was nowhere else in the world I belonged at the moment. The place was packed, the seats filled with friends and relatives of the kids about to get their new dogs. Their buzzy excitement and continuous camera clicks created an exhilarating vibe that echoed off the walls like surround sound in the movies.

We trainers were in the first row center, left to right, Megan, Maria, Lissa, JJ, Trey. And me. We all wore identical rust-colored Canine Connections T-shirts— "No one can really rock rust," as Regan so charmingly pointed out—but the message printed on the back overcame that less-than-attractive color: I SUPPORT COLD NOSES, WARM HEARTS, HAPPY TAILS.

Six examples of the best of those sat obediently at our feet. The dapper dogs had that just-shampooed look, fluffy, soft, clean. Their attire was even less flattering than ours, but the message did, in fact, rock. They wore sage-green reflective vests identifying them as service dogs. Each one—Romeo, Daffodil, Chainsaw, Otis, Clark Kent, and Rex—was highly skilled, obedient, intelligent, loyal. Each was a symbol of hope and unconditional love.

On stage were the winners of a life-changing lottery. Through other eyes, they might have represented a ragtag roundup of kids usually referred to as disabled, handicapped, wheelchair-bound, visually challenged. They appeared broken.

Not to this audience, not in this space, not now. Today, they radiated hope and unshakable belief. This was partly because of us, because of what we had accomplished with our dogs over the past months. Their lives were about to change; they'd soon become more independent, less pitied. More normal.

My heart hurt.

I did not want to be there.

Of course I was proud of Rex—and of myself. I'd even admit to a tinge of excitement. Still, a black cloud hung over me. I couldn't have been more terrified, and that terror threatened to take me down. Knowing I was doing the right thing did not quell the voice in my head that was wailing, *How will I live without Rex?*

The staticky buzz of the switched-on microphone signaled that the ceremony was about to begin. LuLu took the stage. As opposed to her usual dusty jeans, sneakers, and "let's get to work" attitude, she was wearing beige linen pants, pretty pumps, and an ear-to-ear grin. "Welcome, everyone, to graduation day!"

An enthusiastic round of applause greeted her.

"Today," she said, "one journey has ended and another is about to begin. For our trainers"—she paused to acknowledge us—"this is the finish line of a long, sometimes bumpy, but always thrilling road. You had a goal, and now you've reached it. We are all very proud of you, and offer you our deepest thanks."

The applause was heartfelt—and loud. Someone whistled. *Please don't ask us to stand,* I prayed. I slunk down a little in my chair, only to have Mom, sitting directly behind me, tap me on the shoulder. She whispered, "Don't slouch. Be proud of what you did. We are."

Regan, perched next to Mom, was busy taking pictures. Not for any family scrapbooks, nor for me, but to attach to her essay. I had to hand it to the girl—she'd always been on point.

"For our clients, the brave, adventurous group behind me"—LuLu swiveled her neck and smiled at them—

"today marks the first day of the rest of your new, independent, and, we believe, happier lives."

Unsurprisingly, the shout-out to the kids got the biggest applause, rollicking cheers, a standing ovation.

"There's still a lot of work to do," LuLu cautioned. "Starting tomorrow, our recipients and the dogs they've been paired with begin their customized training. You've been through orientation and the learning process. Now, your dogs will come live with you in our dorm. Together, you and your new best friend will learn how to do exactly what *you* need him or her to. The next week will be intense, but it's the time for you to bond."

Was it also the time for me and Rex to "unbond"? Was that possible to do? The boulder in my throat blocked my airway and a tear spilled over my lower eyelid. For the longest time, I couldn't cry. Now, I couldn't stop.

Of course my snap-happy sister picked that exact moment to materialize in front of me and take a picture.

"Delete it!" I whispered angrily.

"No," she assured me, "it's going to be amazing—it'll show how hard it is to give the dog up. It's the perfect narrative to go with my essay. You taught me that!"

Great.

"Let's get this party started!" LuLu exclaimed. "When I call your name, please join me at the microphone. Then

I'll call the trainer of your new dog to hand the leash over to you."

For some reason, right then, I remembered my cousin's wedding, the moment when her parents "handed her off," gave the daughter they'd raised over to her new husband. At the time, I'd seen one family expanding, another shrinking.

It felt very similar.

The ceremony began. The pairings were going as I'd predicted. Megan was the picture of pride and perfection as she regally climbed the few steps to the stage. She handed Romeo over to Hailey, the girl who needed crutches to get around, who wanted to chase boys at recess. Hailey blushed when the handsome chocolate Lab stood next to her.

Daffodil, the yellow Lab, was paired with the wheelchair-bound Kaitlyn. The dog immediately placed her head in Kaitlyn's lap. The girl shrieked with joy. "Mom!" she called. "Look! She already loves me!"

Chainsaw would help Joss, the blind teen, find his way around a new, unfamiliar college campus. They were both beaming.

Otis looked ready to lift the spirits of the sad boy with a respiratory disorder. The kid looked anything but sad right now.

And little Clark Kent, a hoot as usual, bounded up

the steps to meet Daniel, the autistic child. Daniel instantly wraped his bird-like arms around the dog's neck.

There was only one pairing left. Rex had been assigned to Kim, the girl with cerebral palsy. I stood . . . and froze. I could not go through with this.

The room became quiet. I heard my mom's sharp intake of breath and Regan stage-whisper, "Go!" I ignored them. Instead of leading Rex to the stage, I kneeled next to him—this angel who'd seen me through the darkest of days.

And yet somehow I knew. This moment was not for caving in to selfish needs. This was my moment to be brave. Dad trusted I'd know the difference. Somewhere, he still does. I pressed my cheek to Rex's bristly muzzle and whispered, "If you need me, I'm always here."

The tear made it only halfway down my cheek. Rex raised his padded paw and—maybe he'd meant to, maybe it was an accident—wiped it away. I led Rex up to the stage, and that's when I heard it. I would never know if the dog said it or I'd imagined it.

"Say good night, Gracie."

The next moment, Rex was at Kim's feet, her angel now.

·· Epilogue ··

June, one year later

Must you pass *every* car on the road?" I said to Regan—aka Lead Foot—as she raced down the turnpike. "You're going to get a ticket."

"No, I won't," she said, brushing me off. "Anyway, today will go fine. Stop being so nervous."

"I'm not." (I'm lying.)

"Right." She brushed her golden hair over her shoulder.

"And would you mind keeping both hands on the wheel?" I needled her.

Regan's response was to turn up the volume on the radio. I gnashed my teeth. She knew I hated the song.

My relationship with my sister hasn't changed much in a year. She's still a crap driver, and our "carguments" have become legendary. I confess: a part of me is grateful for this return to normalcy. 'Cause it won't last. Regan leaves soon for New York. Yup, she got accepted at Parsons. Her "iWin" streak remains unchallenged. I'm happy for her.

Besides, I couldn't say anything else to annoy her. Regan was doing me a huge favor, agreeing to drive me two and a half hours—each way—to and from Orlando.

Orlando is where Kim lives. I'll be seeing Rex for the first time in a year.

I wasn't just nervous. I was terrified.

Would seeing him remind me how much I missed him? Does he talk to Kim? Would he talk to me? Would he even remember me?

I got the answer to that last question practically the minute I rang the bell. The door swung open and next thing I knew, I was on the floor. Rex couldn't contain himself. The big galumph of a dog went wild at my arrival. His over-greeting involved barking, serious tail action, and launching himself in the air—I know he only meant to put his paws on my shoulders—to say, "I remember you! I love you!" While I was down, he licked my face like an ice-cream cone that was about to melt.

That's how the visit started, everyone belly-laughing at the lunatic dog. Eventually, Rex ran out of steam and we settled down to talk, Kim, her parents, and me.

Reality check: I'd forgotten how odd Kim looked.

Twisting and turning, unable to control her muscles, her head and neck lolled back and forth almost constantly. Her words came out thickly, as if her tongue was in the way. But nothing could prevent her from telling me how much she loved Rex. She glowed the entire time.

Rex really had changed Kim's life. He goes to school with her. He wears a harness for Kim to grasp, which helps her balance. Best of all, the scruffy mutt attracted the attention of her classmates immediately. Rex was his usual friendly self. And once the kids got to know Rex, they got to know Kim—not as someone disabled who made them uncomfortable, but as just another kid at school. Bonus: for the first time in her life, Kim had a best friend.

I listened carefully for any clue about Rex talking. No one mentioned it. Kim and her family were curious about me. What had made me decide to adopt and train him? What was *my* saga?

Rex came to sit by my side. The old habit of stroking that prickly-fuzzy spot on the top of his head between his ears came back to me. Before I knew it, I was telling the whole story. About my dad, about how Rex unexpectedly gave me courage and lots of laughs. He helped me get through the darkest time of my life.

The only thing I failed to mention was the talking-dog bit. Guess that'll stay between me and Rex.

When I finished, Kim looked at her mom excitedly. "Can we give it to her now?" she asked.

Kim's mom nodded and handed her daughter a gift-wrapped package, which Kim instantly thrust at me.

"This is so not necessary!" I protested.

"Open it! Open it!" Kim demanded.

I looked at Rex. I could swear the dog smiled at me.

I can't say whether my tears started before or after Kim's mom explained why they'd given me a present. I can say they trickled all over the wrapping paper.

"You gave us such a gift, Grace. Please accept this as a small token of our appreciation."

Inside was a handmade thank-you note from Kim and a framed certificate that read, "World's Greatest Friend." Next to it was Rex's paw print.

I was too choked up to properly thank them. I kept remembering one of my last "conversations" with Rex. It was during the time when I'd have done anything to keep him. "We'll always be together," the dog had insisted.

Whether Rex was some kind of Dad-reincarnation or had channeled his spirit, I'll never know. But I do know this: The pound dog nailed it. In my heart, he and my dad would be with me forever.

Regan, who'd been out shopping during my visit (what a surprise!) picked me up soon after. My eyes were red and swollen; my nose was running. She took one look and said, "You should wear sunglasses." Then she plucked her own from atop her head and shoved them at me.

They were oversize and trendy. They looked absolutely ridiculous on me. Just like my teary, goofy smile.

Yes, Regan sped all the way home. And nope, she didn't get a ticket.

Acknowledgments

I am so lucky to have Michelle Nagler as my editor-extraordinaire. Any writer would be fortunate to snag her! And to Margaret Miller, who, along with Nagler, did a kickin' editing job. On HB's behalf and my own, thanks to Phyllis Wender, an early believer.

Thanks so much—

To the authorial "firm" of (Helen) Bernstein & (Robin) Wasserman for their knowing encouragement, always.

To the Davies daughters—Danielle, Shannon, and Nicole—and their incredible mom, Ellen, for all their help and musical insight.

To Michael Kassan and Barbara Rubin for sharing eighth-grade curriculums.

To the "group"—my rocks—for their never-ending encouragement and enthusiasm: Karen Berchman, Jane Kalfus, Sharyn Kail, Gay Kassan, Susan Gardner, Alice Goldberg, and Laura Mandelbaum.

To the family: Marvin, Scott, Stefanie, Dan, and

Kathy for putting up with me. And to the babies, Mason and Ruthie, for just being.

To Noogie Reisfeld and Mookie (Bear) Greenberg.

I owe a big debt of gratitude to these organizations who generously allowed me to do "ride-alongs"—to hang out and watch them train their talented dogs to become service dogs. If you ever want to witness miracles in the making, to see how these dedicated pros and volunteers teach dogs to better the lives of physically and mentally challenged kids, adults, and military veterans, check out their websites. Better yet, get involved!

Educated Canines
Assisting with Disabilities
PO Box 251
Dobbs Ferry, NY 10522
www.ecad1.org

Guiding Eyes for the Blind
611 Granite Springs Road
Yorktown Heights, NY 10598
www.guidingeyes.org